OLUSTEE

AMERICA'S UNFINISHED CIVIL WAR BATTLE

GREG AHLGREN

To Debbie,

Enjoy!

Greg Ahlgren 8/8/18

OLUSTEE

AMERICA'S UNFINISHED CIVIL WAR BATTLE

GREG AHLGREN

Canterbury House Publishing

www.canterburyhousepublishing.com
Sarasota, Florida

Canterbury House Publishing

www. canterburyhousepublishing. com

Book Design by Tracy Arendt

Library of Congress Cataloging-in-Publication Data

Names: Ahlgren, Gregory, 1952- author.
Title: Olustee : America's unfinished Civil War battle / Greg Ahlgren.
Description: Sarasota, FL : Canterbury House Publishing, 2018. | Includes
  bibliographical references and index.
Identifiers: LCCN 2017057943 (print) | LCCN 2017059840 (ebook) | ISBN
  9781945401060 | ISBN 9781945401053 (trade pbk. : alk. paper)
Subjects: LCSH: Reporters and reporting--Florida--Fiction.
Classification: LCC PS3601.H563 (ebook) | LCC PS3601.H563 O48 2018 (print)
  |
DDC 813/.6--dc23
LC record available at https://lccn.loc.gov/2017057943

First Printing April 2018

AUTHOR'S NOTE:
This is a work of fiction. Names characters, places and incidents are either the
product of the author's imagination or are used fictiously, and any resemblance to
actual persons living or dead, business establishments, events, or locales is entirely
coincidental.

For information about permission to reproduce selections from this book email:
Canterbury House Publishing, Ltd.
publisher@canterburyhousepublishing.com
Please put Permissions in the subject line

PROLOGUE

"Did you speak to him?"

Edward Dickerson surveyed the visitor standing in his foyer, snow flakes dotting his cloak. The man made no effort to brush them from his clothing, instead keeping his eyes riveted on his host.

He's desperate, Dickerson thought, before turning and leading Marshall Roberts back to his study.

The visitor fell in behind. "You were in Washington for three days. Did you meet with him or not?"

Dickerson motioned to his servant who appeared in the doorway.

"Take Mr. Roberts' outer clothes and dry them by the fire." Dickerson seated himself behind an oak desk.

His visitor fumbled off his cloak and top hat. The servant took the clothes and withdrew, softly closing the study's door behind him.

Dickerson sighed. "Yes, I met with him." He pointed at the stuffed chair opposite his desk. Roberts sat without looking down. He continued to stare straight ahead.

"And?" Roberts demanded.

"These are delicate matters," Dickerson began. "And political."

"Delicate?" Roberts erupted. "There's nothing delicate about that traitor Yulee going into a Confederate court and getting control of my railroad. What kind of nonsense is this? *My* railroad!"

Dickinson shrugged and tilted back in his chair. "Well, he is a one-third owner."

Roberts roared. "With my money!"

"*Our* money," Dickerson corrected.

"*Our* money," Roberts conceded. He waved his arm dismissively. "But mostly mine. You're the lawyer. Need I remind you what's at stake here? It was *The Star of the West* that was fired on bringing supplies to Fort Sumter that started this insurrection. My ship! And the cowards shot at it. A private ship! The only reason that sniveling traitor Yulee was allowed in on this deal was because he was a United States senator from Florida who could get us the permits. Who would have thought he'd throw in with the rebels?"

"Well," Dickerson offered, raising an eyebrow, "he's not the only one down there who's done that. And aren't you forgetting that it was he who started the railroad?"

Roberts slumped back in his seat. "No, I suppose not. But that was eight years ago. It was my money that built the line across Florida."

He shook his head. "Going into a Confederate court and getting control of my railroad—our railroad, sorry—on the basis that you and I are now enemy aliens, why that is just too low, even for a United States senator."

"Former."

"Even worse." Roberts nodded vigorously. "Forget Jeff Davis. It's David Levy Yulee who ought to hang from a sour apple tree when this thing is over."

Dickerson frowned. "You didn't seem to mind his character when he sold us an interest in the railroad, and we all celebrated together in a spirit of fellowship."

Roberts leaned forward. "Yeah, but that was before he snuck into a Confederate court and got those rebel judges to award our interest to him, now, wasn't it?"

"I don't know." Dickerson shrugged. "At some level, you've got to admire a pretty shrewd legal move."

Roberts sat back and chuckled. "Yes, it was. You know, they almost got him in '62 when the *Ottawa* shelled the last train leaving Fernandina. Killed several on board they did, but the traitorous devil himself escaped. At least the Union's held both ends of my rail line ever since."

Marshall Roberts perked up. "See here, Dickerson, did you make it clear how much money's involved? This war has to end sometime. No matter who wins, the whole western part of this continent is going to open up. Immigrants are pouring in to New York and Boston even with the war. Irish, Italians, Poles. You can't walk around New York without hearing jibber-jabbering in some immigrant language on every street corner. Right here in New York! These foreigners have to go someplace. Shipping from New York to New Orleans, and then up the Mississippi, is going to increase ten-fold to fill the demand of those moving west. And my—our—railroad right across Florida, from Fernandina on the Atlantic coast to Cedar Key on the Gulf, why, that saves sailing around Florida. Cuts off eight hundred miles, eliminates a reef or one of those blasted hurricanes sinking one of my ships, lets me ship all year round—a heck of a lot of money at stake here.

"And now there's a Confederate Kangaroo court order saying it's all his?" Roberts shook his head. "This is ridiculous!"

"As you say, the war will end—"

"But not before those rebels dig up my tracks!" Roberts slapped his hand on the desk. "They can't make rails down south, they can't manufacture anything down there. Too incompetent, the whole traitorous lot of them. And iron rails are heavy. Too small a price tag for their blockade runners to bother with. The rebels are desperate for beef now that we've closed the Mississippi. The only way to feed Lee's renegades is to ship beef up from Florida. Do you realize that Florida has more cattle than people, that, and mosquitoes? That's why no one will ever live there, at least, not south of Tampa, mark my words.

"And to get that meat to Lee they have to drive the herds to the Georgia rail yard at Lawton. It's only a matter of time before they realize they need to extend the rails south from the Georgia yards down to Live Oak and ship the herds from there. And where do you think they'll get those rails from, eh Dickerson?"

Marshall Roberts reached inside his jacket and tugged out a thick cigar. Biting off one end he spit the tip toward the spittoon at the side of the desk. Dickerson couldn't see if the tip made it in.

"They've already tried," Dickerson said. "Yulee has stopped the rebels from seizing the rails in the Confederate courts so far. For that matter we'll be lucky if our own government doesn't confiscate our line."

"That's why we have Stickney down there." Roberts pointed the cigar at his host. "To keep paying taxes to the federal collectors and keep our own miserable government from grabbing what's mine."

Dickerson shrugged. "Even if one government or another takes our rails, railroads can be rebuilt, tracks reassembled."

Roberts waved the cigar angrily before putting a match to its tip. He puffed heavily until it glowed red.

"Money, Dickerson, money." Roberts removed the cigar. "And time. When this foolish war ends I want to start shipping right away, not sit around looking for rails that I already paid good money for."

Roberts extended his arm and examined the cigar. Apparently satisfied that it would stay lit, he again pointed it at his host. "So, what did he say? Are they going to help?"

Dickerson slid an ashtray across the desk at his guest. Roberts flicked into it without taking his eyes off the lawyer.

"As I said," Dickerson began, "this is delicate. And political. I met with Mr. Hamlin. But the Vice President is not going to intercede with Lincoln to save a private investment, just for money."

Roberts grunted. "*Just* money? It's not *just* money when it's yours."

Dickerson ignored the jibe. "The president is going to have a tough time this year. People in his own party think he's gone soft and much too far. Freeing the Negroes was one thing, but now there's this constitutional amendment to make them equal, talk of conciliation with the South when this is all over, his own party may not re-nominate him. There's even talk of his running as a Democrat or at least on some combined Democrat-Republican unity ticket."

"So?" Roberts demanded. "What does that have to do with my railroad?"

"As you say, I'm the lawyer. I assume you read the newspapers, Marshall. Last month the President signed the *Proclamation of Amnesty and Reconstruction*. If ten percent of the registered voters of 1860 hold an election in any state currently in rebellion, excepting of course Virginia, and include in their new constitution provisions outlawing slavery, and pledge allegiance to the Union, that state can be re-admitted with full rights."

Roberts eyes narrowed. "And?"

Dickerson sighed. "As you say, of the one hundred sixty-six thousand citizens in Florida in 1860, all but maybe thirty-five hundred live north of Tampa. The Union has held Jacksonville since the fall of '62. The army runs an occasional raid against local militias to capture arms, some cattle. If the federal army drives west out of Jacksonville in force, pushes toward the capital of Tallahassee, why, they could capture enough land to stop the cattle drives and starve Lee, and enough population that they'd be more than enough Unionists to hold an election.

"The Republican nominating convention is in June. With Florida's delegates made up of only those loyal to Lincoln–as well as to the Union–Mr. Lincoln's re-nomination would be all but assured. And with Florida's electoral votes in his column, the President should easily win this November, all without running on some combined Republican-Democrat ticket that is more Democrat than Republican. And I need not tell you as a businessman, Marshall, how much more favorable that will be to us after the war."

Roberts took a long drag and tilted his head back, staring at the ceiling. When he next spoke, he did not look at his host.

"How far out of Jacksonville?"

Dickerson shrugged and laid his hands on his desk, palms down. "Capturing enough land and loyal citizens to make that ten percent also, by pure coincidence, captures the trans-peninsular line of the Florida Railroad Company, protecting the tracks from both rebel scavengers and Florida courts. As I say, our solution is delicate and political."

"The Vice-President, Hamlin, he's been taken care of, eh, I mean he sees the wisdom of this?"

Dickerson nodded. "My original hope was to get Lincoln to approve Congressman Eli Thayer's plan to invade Florida with twenty thousand federal troops, have them become citizens and start raising cotton, and then let them vote in a new state government and give Lincoln his delegates that way. The president liked the plan at one time but can't spare the soldiers. So, we're back to Hamlin.

"The Vice-President indeed sees the wisdom of all this. I made sure he did. And he will speak to the President. The military risk is minimal. Generals Gillmore and Seymour will soon have over six thousand Union soldiers in Jacksonville and the rebel's best units are all up north."

Roberts nodded slowly. "I like it. Now what do we do?"

"It's simple." Dickinson clasped his hands together behind his head. "We wait. Now, may I pour you some of this whiskey?"

CHAPTER 1

Tampa, Florida
Four Days Ago

I was always nervous when my editor asked me into his office. I never knew if he was going to give me a new assignment or fire me, which is more of a comment on the state of journalism now-a-days than my writing skills.

Mark Whigham did not look up when I entered, which I took as a good sign. I sprawled in one of the two vinyl chairs facing his desk and waited. He moved the mouse one way, then another, then appeared to circle it before left clicking it. He closed his laptop enough that we could make eye contact.

"Jason, my boy, what do you have going?" He peered over his glasses.

"Not much." I shrugged. "I'm working on the school budget fight. I covered the public hearing last night and put the article to bed. I want to follow up with some teachers. Long range, I'm working on a two or three-part article on a Sarasota cold case murder from the eighties. The two college students found wrapped in plastic."

Mark nodded absently. "Haven't we done that one before?"

I repressed a smile. "Yup. Every seven or eight years. It always generates a bit of discussion on the forums, sometimes a few crazy tips that we cobble into a few other stories. I wasn't here last time you did it."

I didn't add that it was he who had suggested the series three weeks earlier. If Mark recalled, he didn't show it. Instead, he got to the reason he summoned me.

"How'd you like to go up north for a couple of days?"

"Sure, why not? Boston, New York, D.C.? Back home to Detroit?"

He frowned. "I know you've got that job application pending. Although why anyone would want to go to Detroit beats me.

You do realize it's in Michigan, right? But no, I was thinking of someplace in-state. You ever hear of a town called Olustee?"

I struggled to hide my ignorance.

"In the panhandle, isn't it?" I held my breath. If it was "up north" yet still in Florida, the panhandle was as safe a guess as any. Anywhere further south would not require "a couple of days."

"Not quite. More like tucked into the northeast corner, just below the Georgia border. A bit west and a tad north of Jacksonville."

When I didn't say anything, he continued.

"There was a Civil War battle fought there."

"I doubt the survivors are talking to the press." I recalled he was some sort of history buff, so I resolved to play nice. If he was offended by my flippancy his face didn't betray it.

"I assume you studied American history in fourth grade up in the Motor City like everyone else."

I did a quick calculation. "That was twenty-one years ago."

"Well, hopefully you didn't forget too much when you went to college. Even at Northwestern they must cover history." He cleared his throat and sat up a bit.

"It was Florida's largest Civil War battle. Union forces captured Jacksonville in '62, and a couple of years later they decided to capture Tallahassee and close down the state to the Confederacy."

"And this is current news because…? Let me guess, you want me to cover some reenactment? Bugles blaring, Lost Cause, South will rise again!"

Mark chuckled. "It's a current battle. The first Battle of Olustee happened in February of 1864, so we just missed this year's re-enactment by a couple of months. Although, I think they did have one.

"No, apparently there are some Confederate monuments that got erected around the beginning of the last century. There's a state park and a national one too. There's a group called the Sons of Union Veterans of the Civil War who want to erect a monument or obelisk or some such thing honoring their Union ancestors, and the local chapter of the Sons of Confederate Veterans are up in arms over it."

"Because...?"

"You know what they say. 'In Florida, the farther north you go...'"

"'...the further south you get.'" I leaned in closer, laughing. He laughed with me.

"Anyway." He grew serious and glanced at the clock on the wall behind me. "Go up and poke around. The Florida Department of Parks is holding a public hearing tomorrow on the request to gauge local input. Then some yahoos in the legislature are holding a public hearing there the next day on a bill to strip the Parks Department of the right to decide where monuments go— an end run. I guess they figure the Parks Department decision will go badly for the Stars and Bars crowd. Snoop around, sit in on both hearings, talk to some locals, try to get an outrageous quote or two. Couple of pictures. Maybe a background fluff piece on the battle if you're so inclined."

I nodded and stood up. "I'll find a local with a long pointy beard."

As I turned to the door Mark added one last admonition.

"Three nights, that's it. Nothing more expensive than a Motel Six."

"Who knows," I shot back over my shoulder, "maybe I'll camp out on the battlefield."

Three days ago

The next day I drove three hours and a little under 200 miles north from Tampa. A cultural light-year away. Not a bad car ride, however, and it gave me a chance to reflect on the assignment when I wasn't watching for Florida Highway Patrol cruisers tucked behind billboards.

I had spent the rest of the previous afternoon doing a bit of research on the battle, and the current monument controversy.

Nothing heavy, some basic Googling and Wikipedia stuff. When you write for an on-line magazine—e-zine we call it—that's often all you need.

I'd been out of school eight years and was still bouncing around the writing biz. After college I came down to take some graduate classes and soak up the sunshine, not necessarily in that order. I worked for newspapers in Sarasota and Tampa, but e-writing gave me a whole new platform. Besides, if I screwed up a fact, or forgot a comma, e-writing let me correct it.

The Sun Coast News and Observer was an e-zine comprised of arts features such as theatrical and book reviews, some sports columns on the Tampa pro teams and USF, and the odd human-interest story. Ignored military veterans was a favorite of Mark's.

The where-are-they-now column was a staple, and what had led me into a couple of cold case two-parters, including the one I had been working on when summoned into Mark's office the day before.

That was another thing. Most e-zines didn't have offices—didn't need them—but I figured Mark and his co-owner wanted a place to hang out during the day. Closer to the downtown diners they both loved.

But, I thought, as I plunged north, it might soon all be coming to an end. I had applied for an opening as a political reporter at the Detroit Free Press, the interviews had gone well, I knew the editor, and it was all looking good. I expected the official call any day. Perhaps soon there would be no more fluff pieces.

The complicating factor was Anne. A middle school social studies teacher, she was smart and funny, and I was crazy in love with her. She was also the divorced mother of a five-year-old daughter, Cameron. Returning to Detroit would end our relationship. Oh, she'd love to move from Tampa to Detroit—who wouldn't, especially in the winter? But being a divorced mom of a five-year-old whose custody she shared with her ex meant no court in Florida was going to let her take the kid to live out of state. She could move to Detroit all right—by herself. No way she'd ever do that, and no way I'd ask her to.

I stopped for lunch in Gainesville, took a quick tour around my old never-finished grad school stomping grounds, marveled at how much younger the co-eds were getting, and got back on the road. The Florida Department of Parks had scheduled a four o'clock public hearing in a local elementary school, and I didn't want to be late.

I found the school with no problem, and a bored security guard pointed at the auditorium without asking who I was. So much for school security.

The auditorium doubled as the school gym. For this event they'd set up folding metal chairs opposite a table with a microphone. A podium at the front of the makeshift center aisle faced the table. Arriving early gave me a chance to pick a spot in the right corner up front, close to both the podium and the table. I opened my steno pad and waited. Yes, I have a laptop, but I can scribble faster than I can hunt and peck. Besides, I liked the old-time image it projected. I often pictured myself wearing a fedora with a "Press" card tucked in the band.

The room filled slowly, and I fantasized a back story for each entrant. Just before four a short, nervous-looking man in his late forties wearing Dockers and an open dress shirt bustled behind the table. He whispered with two women while shooting furtive glances over the swelling crowd. This was my cue. I approached the trio and introduced myself as Jason Bauman. I told them I was covering the hearing for my magazine and that I might be taking pictures. When you tell as opposed to asking, you never get push back. Freedom of the press and all that. The nervous man frowned but offered neither a name nor an objection.

At four he called the meeting to order and introduced himself as an assistant director of the Florida Parks Department. He explained that state law required public hearings on all requested proposals near the area most affected. He then read a state law from a document he held that appeared to say the same thing. He announced that a proposal had been made to his department by an organization called Sons of Union Veterans of the Civil War to erect a monument in the state park—here he resorted to reading the official proposal—at their expense honoring Union soldiers who had fought at the Battle of Olustee.

He introduced the two women as fellow department employees and emphasized that no decision would be made that day. In fact, the three employees had no authority to make one. Today was merely an opportunity for public input. All comments and feedback would be taken back to the Department, which would then have final say. He didn't say who exactly would make that decision. Since the proposal came from a private organization he would allow their representative to speak first, outlining the proposal, before he opened up comments to the general public.

A balding man with white hair, sporting a navy blazer, blue shirt and red tie, approached the podium. He looked to be in his sixties. His right hand held one of those Civil War caps you see in the movies, which he placed atop the podium. I scribbled a quick reminder that those caps had to have a name and I'd better get it right for the story.

He introduced himself as William Dunleavy, a retired case manager at the U.S. Department of Health and Human Services. He was also the commander of the local camp of the Sons of Union Veterans of the Civil War, a Congressionally chartered organization open to any male who had an ancestor who had fought for the Union and been killed or honorably discharged.

I made another note to find out what a Congressionally chartered organization was.

He talked about his ancestor, who had nothing to do with the Battle of Olustee. However, living locally, Dunleavy had toured the battle site on many occasions. A few times a year he was approached by visitors whose ancestors fought in the battle, and he often accompanied them around the area. Although there were at least three Confederate monuments in the three-acre state park, none honored the Union soldiers who had fought and died to preserve the Union and end slavery, a fact inevitably brought up by those he escorted. The national organization had raised funds to build a monument, and he thought it high time one was set there. He talked about the beauty of Gettysburg, where monuments from both sides honored those who had fought so bravely on that Pennsylvania farm.

He was the only speaker in favor. It was downhill after that.

The next speaker was from the local chapter of the Sons of Confederate Veterans, and he talked about the courage and bravery of the Floridians who had resisted what he termed "The War of Northern Aggression." Erecting a monument on Florida land, dedicated to the aggressors who had fought *against* Florida, would be an affront to the sacrifice of these brave Floridians and their Georgian brethren.

The third speaker appeared in the full Confederate military dress of a captain, and likened erecting a monument to the Union soldiers to erecting a monument to Al-Qaeda at Ground Zero in New York City.

A fourth argued that the Confederate men who fought for the principle of states rights did so out of pure loyalty to their governor, who had asked them to enlist to protect their state, and he was sick and tired of Confederates being considered by some as traitors.

"Most of these people who come down here to Florida aren't even from Florida." I quickly scribbled to try to keep up. "They come from up North with their Northern ideas and Northern values and try to impose them on us."

I was reminded of the line Mark and I had laughed over the day before about the farther north you go in Florida. I wondered if I could get one of the speakers to repeat it for inclusion in my article, attributed to one of the participants.

At the conclusion, the panel said little, other than that they'd be bringing the ideas expressed back to their department for consideration. The chairman did reference that the legislature was going to hold a subcommittee hearing on changing the law the next day at the same location and invited everyone who had an interest to return. Then the three beat it out a rear door.

The rest of us filed out the front to the parking lot, with the Confederate group huddling together at one end. I passed them with a nod, and hurried after Dunleavy, catching him as he entered his car.

I established his name and address and learned that he described himself as an S.O.B.—Sons of Both. He was a member of the Sons of Union Veterans of the Civil War and a member of the Sons of Confederate Veterans—they never used the term Civil War.

After telling me to call him Bill, he said he was on his way home—his wife Alice was ill with the flu—but he promised he'd be back the next day and we'd talk more. He asked if I'd toured the battlefield. When I indicated I had not, he gave me directions and shook his head. "Google map won't get it right."

I figured I'd get statements from the opponents the next day and headed west toward the battle site. I'd need pictures of the present monuments, and I wanted to catch the light while I could. Besides, what better quotes could I get than the ones I'd heard?

Following Bill's directions, I headed out along Route 90. Turning north off the highway I bumped across railroad tracks and into the parking area. Admission to the park was free, and I eased my BMW to a spot near the small Visitors Center that stood in the middle of a clearing. The surrounding terrain was thick with pine. Dunleavy said there were three Confederate monuments behind the building, the first erected in 1912 by the Daughters of the Confederacy. Locking my car with a chirp, I followed his directions and circled around the building on foot. I was not alone.

An elderly woman knelt in front of an obelisk, tending a Boxwood plant. It was too good a shot to miss, and I hoisted my camera and clicked away before approaching. A quote from a local civilian was missing from my story, and I might be in luck.

She stood and turned as I approached, brushing her trousers before wiping her hands on a towel. I figured her to be about seventy-five years old. She was dressed in baggy khakis and her head was wrapped in a bright kerchief. I introduced myself and told her my mission.

She nodded. "Covering the ruckus at the school, are you?" In a strong voice she told me her name was Agnes Thornberry, admitting she lived nearby.

This could be good. "It's a beautiful monument." I stepped back, looking up. I hoped to allay suspicion.

She squinted, raising her hand as a visor to shield the setting sun behind me.

I read the inscription aloud. "Here was fought on February 20, 1864 the Battle of Ocean Pond under the immediate command of General Alfred Holt Colquit, the 'Hero of Olustee.'"

She turned back to the monument as I continued. "'Erected April 20, 1936 by the Alfred Holt Colquit Chapter United Daughters of the Confederacy, Georgia Division.'"

I nodded solemnly when I finished. "Impressive."

This was one of the three monuments the opposing speakers maintained already commemorated the battle, rendering superfluous any Union ones.

"Are you a member of the Georgia Division of the Daughters of the Confederacy?" I was impatient to start a conversation.

"Georgia?" The woman shook her head and chuckled. "No, I'm one of the few Floridians that I'm sure you heard all about at the school, several generations we are."

"Ah, a real native. Do you have a connection with the monument?"

The woman shrugged, and stooped again, using a trowel to press dirt around the plant.

When she stood again she turned full to me.

"My family has lived and worked this land for generations. My great-grandmother did her damnedest to keep the farm afloat during the war that all them at the school you just left love to beat their chests over. If you really want a story for your newspaper, Mr. Bauman, why don't you try writing hers? My grandmother remembered it to me almost every day when I was a child. I hung on every word, and it was as if she was telling me things about her own mother that happened yesterday. And it always started on that crisp day in February, in the fourth year of the Great War as she called it, when a dust covered stranger in a gray uniform ambled down the road to the farm just as her mother was finishing her work for the day."

CHAPTER 2

Miriam Aggafor moved the milk pail back behind her stool and stood up. Once, she had stood before moving the pail, only to have the cow kick out, cascading an evening's work across the barn's dirt floor. She never repeated her mistake.

Moving the stool further back, she carried the pail to the far wall before returning to untie the twin halters. Clucking as loudly as she could, she led the cow back to the tie rail to join the three that had already been milked for the night. She carried the pail outside, then latched the barn door.

She looked again at the rough-hewn door of vertical pine slats. Like the barn itself, covered in whitewash, it looked ridiculous. The paint had long ago peeled and cracked, but getting new wash was near impossible now, even if Papa or Johnny were still around to paint it. And the slats were spaced too far apart, allowing small animals to wedge between them.

It wasn't only animals she needed to keep out. Rustlers, deserters and draft evaders now filled the surrounding countryside. Located forty miles west of Jacksonville, the terrain around Sanderson was as good a place as any in Florida for someone who wished not to be found.

It had been safer when Papa was alive. Besides, before the war, there was no place for a criminal to go, even if someone tried to rustle the farm's herd of cattle.

But that didn't matter anymore. Every beef herd in Northern Florida had long since been sold to the Confederate Army to the north. The only time Miriam saw beef cattle now was when the crackers drove long herds from below Tampa past their farm up to the Georgia rail yards.

Miriam was left with four cows and a bull on a 28-acre tomato, bean and beet farm she managed herself. Or at least since Johnny had succumbed to the urge to run off and join the fight. And her brother would not be coming back to help her. A Union Minié ball at Chickamauga the prior September assured that.

Using the back of her right hand she wiped the sweat from her brow and grunted as she hoisted both milk containers. She couldn't rely much on the slave who was left. Hanna belonged to her uncle, Jacob Samuels, who had entrusted her to Miriam and her mother when he left his own adjacent farm to join Robert Hoke and his Carolinians. The one male slave who had helped Papa before the war ran off to Jacksonville as soon as it fell to the Yankees two years earlier. The last Miriam heard, he'd joined the Union Navy as a coal heaver.

Hanna helped in the field, but the Negress would have nothing to do with cows. Papa, or even Johnny, could have taught Hanna better, but that wasn't going to happen now, and Miriam's mother hardly ever left her room anymore.

At the door to the farmhouse Miriam lowered the twin pails to the porch floor and undid the latch. Then movement caught her eye. She turned to watch a solitary figure trudge down the road from the west. His tattered and dust-caked clothes were shaded in the unmistakable gray of the Confederate Army. He carried no rifle and bore no backpack. A deserter. She searched his waist for a pistol or sword but saw neither. It was the ones still carrying weapons you had to worry about.

Sometimes she carried Papa's loaded Enfield around the barnyard. Tonight she'd left it in a kitchen corner for the evening milking. She glanced through the door and calculated. She wouldn't have time to grab it.

Hanna knelt at the tomato plants fifty yards away, pulling weeds, oblivious to the stranger's approach. Four years ago, Miriam would not have been concerned by the man, but four years ago Papa and Johnny were still alive. Now there was just the two white women and Hanna. She resolved to be decisive.

Miriam stepped off the porch and strode toward the stranger with as much confidence as she could muster.

"Can I help you?" She stopped a few feet away.

He removed his hat, a wide-brimmed affair that was clearly not military issue. She noted the arm patches evidencing his rank had been ripped from his sleeves. She took the hat removal as a good sign.

"Ma'am, I'm just passing through, and was looking for a kind face and maybe a meal."

They all wanted a meal. This was a farm, not an inn, and she was always tempted to refuse them. In the end she never did, reasoning such a course might be riskier. Besides, what if it were her uncle, or had been Johnny?

She looked behind him, searching for comrades.

Perhaps sensing hesitation, he added, "I can pay."

"Pay?" The offer surprised her. No one ever offered to pay. Deserters had no money, and if they did, never offered it.

"Yes, ma'am. Not scrip neither, Yankee money."

Not only a deserter, but a thief. Where else would he have gotten Yankee dollars? Still, money was money. If he'd intended her harm he wouldn't have offered.

"We don't have much." She indicated the slave still weeding in the field. "Set yourself in the barn and I'll have Hanna bring you some food in a bit."

His eyes followed hers to the field. "Your sister?"

For the second time that day she was startled. "Sister?" Her eyes flew incredulously to Hanna.

The stranger squinted hard toward where the slave knelt. "I'm sorry, ma'am. No offense meant. Been walking in the sun all day. But she's so light."

It was true enough. Hanna was light skinned. Miriam remembered someone at her uncle's farm remarking as such years earlier, when her parents brought her over for one of their Sunday visits with her mother's brother. At 24, Hanna was only a year older than Miriam. As children they had played together at Uncle

Jacob's farm, sometimes even inside the farmhouse. But as they grew older, they had learned their places.

"No offense taken."

She studied the visitor. Usually deserters kept their kepi caps, the Napoleonic military cap worn by both North and South, differentiated only by color. The kepis offered cover from the sun, and when their folds were extended they provided a deep pouch for foraging. Yet this one wore a soft, wide brimmed hat.

"What unit you from?"

The man hesitated, and she suspected she was about to hear a lie.

"From up Georgia way."

There was no use seeking clarification of a fabrication. "You walk all the way down here? You from Florida?"

She bit her lip. She knew better than to challenge a stranger, what with her standing here and the Enfield inside, but he didn't seem the type who'd try something. Besides, he was older than the boys that ran past, escaping the fighting, looking for a place to hide for the duration. She estimated him to be in his late twenties.

He turned and surveyed the fields, now ripe with winter crops.

"I'm just looking for a place to rest awhile." He turned back to her. "Maybe get myself some work."

"Well, there's no work here." She kept her voice stern. "Go set in that barn and Hanna will bring you some cornmeal and beans. In the morning you best be off."

She took a few steps toward the house before turning back. "And be sure to latch the barn door good behind you. Never can tell what kind of animals are trying to get in."

CHAPTER 3

Samuels-Aggafor Farm
Saturday, February 13, 1864

"Are you the only one who does the milking?"

Miriam spun quickly. She searched the hay and the stalls but didn't spot him. She assumed he had moved on before first light. Deserters liked to keep moving lest they got caught or turned in, and they tended to shy away from farms and settlements. Most who passed through headed for the deeper pines to the west. Some turned south to where few others lived.

She spotted him when he rose up from the straw. He had a new blanket against the night chill. Hanna must have given it to him when she brought the cornmeal.

"I don't think we introduced ourselves proper yesterday." Straw tumbled off him to the ground. "Frederick Mallory." He nodded and smiled.

He must have hidden all night. Even her two horses in the adjacent stalls didn't appear bothered by his presence.

"You're not staying long enough for me to remember you." Miriam tried to keep her tone icy as the morning air.

"Well, I dunno'." He stepped from the straw pile and brushed his clothes. "That slave last night said you could use a bit of man help, what with your father dead and your brother gone."

"My brother's dead. Killed at Chickamauga." Maybe she could shame him into leaving.

He nodded. "I know. She told me."

"We get by just fine here." She turned to the tie rail. The cows were beginning to moo. She saw no reason to encourage a conversation.

He followed her, but not in a way where she felt threatened.

"And Hanna best learn to keep her mouth shut about our farm business," she added. "If she knows what's good for her. I'll take a switch to her myself."

He reached in front of her and untied the nearest cow. He tugged the bovine over to the milking station and attached both halters as Miriam watched.

"I doubt you really mean that, seeing she's not even your own slave, belonging to your uncle next door who's also away."

"Reckon Hanna and you had a good old chat last night, did you?"

He shrugged before retrieving the pail from where Miriam had dropped it.

"Not much else for her to do. And it's tough, what with her being half house slave to you and your mother, and half field hand."

"This ain't no Virginia plantation. We get by with everyone doing what they can."

He grabbed the stool and began expertly tugging on the cow's udders.

Miriam stood to the side. She was offended that he was still here but pleased that she might escape the morning milking.

"Well, I figure I could give you a hand for a bit. Not long. Get you caught up in the field. I see you trying to bring in those winter tomatoes. Beans too."

He wasn't pushy. Deserter or no, he must have done some fighting. Maybe he deserved the truth.

"I got no money," she blurted. "To pay you. Least not 'til I get these crops to market."

He snickered. "I didn't 'spect you had any money. I have a little myself, probably more than you. Yankee dollars, too. But I need a place to stay."

Without removing his hands from the udders, he nodded toward the pile of straw where he had slept. "That's good enough for the work. That and whatever Hanna bring me twice a day, breakfast and supper. Lunch too if it's not much bother."

She bit her lip. It was tempting.

"Where're you bringing your winter crops?"

"Jacksonville."

He half turned and raised an eyebrow.

"I don't care if they're Yankees." She placed her hands on her hips. "Their money's good."

"I got no problem selling food to Union soldiers. They going to eat anyway, and it might as well be a Southern woman who gets the money for it."

He finished with the first cow. She noted that he moved the milk pail behind him before standing and untying the halters.

"Besides, I don't exactly have the right to object to any man eating now, North or South, do I?"

"Where'd you learn farming?"

"Outside Atlanta. If you want, why don't I help you load up and bring your crops into town? Can't be an easy trip by yourself. And you can't exactly bring Hanna into a Union city now, can you? Not if you expect her to come home with you." He chuckled.

She grimaced. "You're a fine one to talk. You going to waltz right into Jacksonville wearing that Confederate uniform? They'll lock you up as a prisoner.

"And no!" she exclaimed, growing hot. "Don't you think you're going to borrow any of Papa or Johnny's clothes."

He shook his head. "I ain't aiming to borrow anything not rightfully mine. But I could get a job scouting for them federals, I heard they hire deserters."

So, he admitted he was a deserter! Well, he was more truthful than she'd expected.

"How far is Jacksonville from here, anyway?" he asked.

"Just over forty miles. We're just to the west of Sanderson. I can ride it in a day if I start early. Two if I have a pair pull a loaded wagon."

He stepped back and whistled. "You can ride forty in a day?"

She smirked. "I'm not one of your Georgia belles walking around with a parasol, Mister?"

"Mallory. Frederick Mallory." He extended his hand. "You seemed to think earlier you had no need for my name."

She ignored the hand. "My father had Johnny and me riding when we could barely toddle. Before the war we had a full beef herd, and always eight or ten horses, good ones too. I can ride as well as anyone."

"I believe you." He lowered his hand. He held them both out, palms up. "But riding overnight by yourself, with a full wagon, even riding saddle all day from here to Jacksonville, why, it can't be all that safe."

"My papa also taught me to shoot, Mr. Mallory."

She stood back and studied his face. "I tell you what. You seem able to handle yourself around a farm. You finish milking and help Hanna load the wagon, you can come with me at first light, day after. But I tell you Mr. Mallory, if some Union sentry shoots you the minute he sees those gray rags on your shoulders, don't be looking to me to bandage or bury you."

"Ma'am," he said, touching the brim of his hat, "I wouldn't dream of it."

CHAPTER 4

8th Regiment, United States Colored Troops
Encampment, Barber Plantation
28 miles west of Jacksonville
12 miles east of Sanderson
Monday, February 15, 1864

"Another sutler's here."

Private Charles Dunhill looked up from the campfire toward where Corporal Thomas Cotton pointed. The day was chilly, and he wanted to stay near the fire as long as possible.

Still, the lure of fresh vegetables, or even meat, was tempting.

Sutlers never had enough, and their supplies were often sold to the soldiers quickest to the wagon. Blue-clad men trotted to where the driver slowed the team. These sutlers had obviously talked their way past the Union sentries. With their sentries, that wasn't surprising.

Corporal Cotton jogged toward the wagon, abandoning his sizzling frying pan. Charles Dunhill rose slowly, brushed the soil from his trousers, and ambled over to the local merchants.

This wagon was different. A young woman tugged back on the reins, coaxing the horses to a stop. Beside her sat a man wearing the tatters of a Confederate uniform.

"Why lookee'," a Union soldier called out as he approached. "Another reb done give up the fight."

Dunhill recognized the speaker, a white boy from the 7th Connecticut Infantry Regiment. Along with the New Hampshire 7th, and his own 8th Regiment, United States Colored Troops, the three regiments had camped at the western end of Barber Plantation for almost a week. Occasionally they had ventured further west to raid Confederate supplies and ammunition. There were other regiments camped at the plantation, but the three regiments of Hawley's Brigade camped together.

The former rebel jumped down from the wagon and faced the Yankee. He held his hands up, palms out.

"I'm not here to fight. Just looking for work."

"What you got?" Corporal Cotton demanded, pushing past the white soldier. Quicker soldiers were already crawling over the wagon, lifting and inspecting sacks stacked along the floorboards.

"Tomatoes!" a soldier exclaimed. "We going to walk across Florida on tomatoes?" Several soldiers laughed.

"We have beans, too," the Confederate said. "Some beets."

Union soldiers selected vegetables and haggled cash prices with the woman.

"Where you from? Around here?" another Yankee asked her.

"Sanderson." The woman pushed the hair off her forehead. Cold or not, driving a team was hard work, and the woman was sweating.

"Sanderson!" another exclaimed. "How far is that?"

The rebel soldier considered. "Maybe ten, twelve miles."

The Yankee whistled. "Aways. Before Lake City?"

The woman nodded. "Can't get to Lake City without marching through Sanderson, and right past my farm."

"Hey reb," a tall white soldier asked, "is your army still at Lake City? That's what we all hear."

"I'm not from there, but it could be," Mallory answered. "I was up Georgia way."

Corporal Cotton nodded. "If you're looking for work, reb, General Truman Seymour, why he been hiring former rebs as scouts. If you know the area."

"You have to take a loyalty oath, though," Dunhill interjected. "All rebel deserters have to take a loyalty oath before getting hired. General Seymour's rules. But he'll pay in Yankee dollars."

"How much? I could use some money."

"Well, you ought to get rid of that uniform first," the tall soldier answered, starting another round of laughter. "The general has five or six former rebs scouting even now."

"Don't seem right," the first white soldier from the Connecticut 7th added. He moved closer to the wagon and placed his hands on his hips. "Why should we be paying them that a few weeks ago just as soon killed us?

"Or maybe," he added, edging up to the newcomer, "we should just shoot you for a spy, coming in here still wearing gray."

The other soldiers grew quiet, and the one standing on the wagon with his arm outstretched, holding cash, froze. Other soldiers backed away.

"I don't want trouble," Mallory repeated.

When Charles Dunhill spotted the white soldier's hand slide toward the knife in his belt he pushed between the pair and faced his Union comrade.

"Leave him be. He don't got no weapon. You can't stick a man with no weapon for wearing gray."

The white soldier started to speak before his eyes traveled past Dunhill. Corporal Cotton jumped off the wagon, his kepi filled with the beets and tomatoes he'd bought, and stood next to Charles.

The white soldier hesitated, and then shrugged.

"Fine, you niggers want to buy from rebs, go ahead." He turned and walked back toward his regiment's neat white rows of tents.

"Let's get out of here." Corporal Cotton grabbed the private by the arm. He pushed Charles Dunhill roughly back toward their fire.

They walked several feet before the corporal turned.

"Are you crazy? What do you want to get mixed up in that for? You could have got knifed. Them Connecticut boys been scrapping with each other all week, since half their regiment left on furlough. One of them boys done stuck one of his own with a knife. Could have been this one that done the sticking."

Charles shrugged and resumed walking. "He was going to kill him. He was reaching for his knife."

"Well, maybe he was right. Two weeks ago, that reb would have shot you dead, weapon or no."

"That be two weeks ago. He's not fighting now. He got no rifle, not even a knife. Getting cut down for no reason ain't right."

Thomas Cotton scoffed. "You fellas' that was born free up in Pennsylvania, you got some notion of white man justice. But down in Virginia, 'afore I escaped north, if a fight broke out between two white men, there be no reason for me to do something. I would sure enough turn and not even see it."

"That's what we're trying to change, ain't it?"

"Or mebbe' you being half-white gives you some special way of seeing things that seem plain to me the other way."

The pair reached their cook fire, still burning hot. Soldiers from their regiment sat on the ground, warming their hands.

Corporal Cotton extended his kepi filled with fresh fruit. "Anyone wanting fresh smoked tomatoes go ahead and take some."

CHAPTER 5

Sergeant Richard Colburn led the group of five new Union recruits across the furrowed fields and into the pine woods at the northern end of Barber Plantation. He walked behind them, carefully studying how they carried their muskets.

"What's your name, lad?" he asked the one directly in front of him.

"Henry Frink, sir!"

"It's Henry Frink, *Sergeant*. Where you from?"

"Chester, New Hampshire, Sergeant."

"Well, we're all from New Hampshire. You do a lot of duck hunting over there in Chester?"

"Yes, Sergeant, most every fall. With my brothers."

"Well, you're not duck hunting now, and that's not a shotgun. Put that rifle on your shoulder."

The boy shifted the Springfield onto his right shoulder. Another recruit who had been carrying his rifle out in front with both hands also shifted his weapon. A third soldier carrying the rifle across his chest did not alter his grip.

"What's your name?" the sergeant asked him.

The soldier stared at Colburn blankly.

"It's Lambert, Sergeant," Frink answered. "I think his first name is Alphonse. I got that much out of him on the boat down. He joined up with us in Manchester. But he don't speak no English."

"What?" The sergeant's eyes flew to the other four. "Any of you others don't speak no English?"

"Just him," Frink answered. The other three nodded.

"He's from Canada," Frink continued. "Works for the Amoskeag Mills in Manchester. Runs a loom. Not much work now that they can't get as much cotton these past years. I think he's a substitute."

"Substitute? For who?" the sergeant demanded.

Another soldier twisted around. "Not sure. I think he was paid by a newspaperman in Manchester to go instead."

"And he obliged because there was not as much cotton?"

The third soldier laughed. "There was a fella' on the boat, another Canuck, spoke his language. Said Lambert here had no idea what he was signing up for when he took the money. The newspaperman just walked him down to the train depot and enlisted him as his substitute."

"Jesus, Mary and Joseph," the sergeant said.

Sergeant Colburn halted the group at a grass clearing. He moved to the front and arranged the soldiers in line. "How many of you had training at one of the camps before shipping south?"

No one responded.

"Well, how many of you been in a militia, maybe your town parade drills?"

Again, no one spoke, and two shook their heads.

"When we enlisted they said we be needed down here right away," Frink volunteered. "Everyone back home be real proud of the Seventh, and me being from Chester, and well, Colonel Bell, he be from Chester too."

Sergeant Colburn nodded. "Your family know Colonel Bell's family?"

"No, sir." Frink blushed. "The Bells live the other side. In a big house."

Sergeant Colburn grunted. "Well, son, it don't matter here what size house you come from."

"They told us what with the Seventh losing so many men, that we be needed and they say we'd get training here," another said.

"And besides," Frink added. "We wanted to get down here while there was still fighting. We was a-feared the rebs would all quit before we could get here. I joined up on my 18ᵗʰ birthday."

"Which was?"

"Almost three weeks ago," Frink answered proudly.

"I don't think you'll have to worry about this war ending too soon."

Taking Private Lambert's rifle, Sergeant Colburn held it in front of the group.

"When the firing starts you men be lined up, shoulder to shoulder. You fire only on command, from the lieutenant or another officer. Sometimes the command might come from me. When you fire, you do so in a direct line, all at once, at the enemy directly in front of you. After you fire you step back, another line of men with loaded rifles will step up and take your place, and they'll fire while you reload.

"Don't worry about forgetting, or not knowing what to do. The Seventh Regiment has been through a number of battles. The men here are good soldiers. We supported the 54ᵗʰ Massachusetts in the attack on Fort Wagner. If you watch the man next to you and do what he does, you'll do fine.

"Now I know you men just arrived by ship in Jacksonville two days ago and marched out here yesterday. But the Seventh shipped down to Jacksonville nine days ago, and we been out here at Barber Plantation for a week. We've done some raids, grabbing arms and food supplies from the Confederates. No idea how long we'll stay here, or when we'll head back to Jacksonville.

"Just last December, boys, someone got the great idea to put the Seventh on horseback, as mounted infantry. I guess they figured anyone from New Hampshire can ride good enough, and they done give us all Spencer repeating carbines, just like the cavalry, and we traded them our Springfields. Great rifles, the Spencers. Shorter barrel, less weight, easier to handle, and the lever-action lets you fire seven cartridges before you reload. And when you do, you just put seven cartridges into the stock. Why, it gives ten men the firepower of seventy a-carrying Springfield muskets."

The sergeant held Private Lambert's rifle aloft with both arms.

"As you can see, this ain't no Spencer repeating rifle I'm holding. When we got to Florida there weren't no horses for us Seventh to ride on. They only had enough horses for the Massachusetts 40th, so they made us trade most of our Spencers to them Massachusetts boys for their Springfields, and now our own Springfields are gone, and we got what the 40th give us in exchange."

He dropped the rifle's stock to the ground, holding it with his left hand, barrel pointing skyward. With his right he reached into his ammunition pouch on his belt and extracted a paper cartridge filled with pre-measured gunpowder and a .58 caliber Minié ball. Ripping open the top of the package with his teeth he poured the powder and ball down the barrel, shoving the paper in on top. He pulled the ramrod from the sling beneath the barrel and tamped down the powder, ball and paper. He then replaced the ramrod into the sling.

Hoisting the rifle with his left hand he reached into a second pouch and retrieved a percussion cap. He half cocked the hammer and placed the percussion cap on the firing nipple.

"All right men, you do the same, but slow, so I can watch you." He kept Private Lambert's rifle and studied the other four.

As they stumbled through the procedure he stopped each one, corrected any misstep as the others watched, and then commanded them to continue. When satisfied that all four rifles were loaded, he positioned the men so they faced away from the encampment. Then he told them to cock their rifle, directing them to aim at the base of a clump of bushes sixty yards away.

"On my command," he said, and the four leveled their rifles at eye height. He handed Private Lambert back his own rifle, and the Canadian imitated his fellow soldiers.

Well, at least he's willing, the sergeant mused before shouting, "Fire!"

Three out of the five rifles discharged, while the hammers of two rifles clicked harmlessly. The two soldiers whose rifles had not discharged stared at them dumbly.

The sergeant swore and grabbed Private Frink's. Holding it with his left hand he removed the untouched percussion cap and manipulated the hammer up and down with his right.

"Hammer's bent," he announced.

"Can it be fixed?" Frink asked, peering over the sergeant's shoulder.

Colburn shook his head. "The pivot pin is bent inside the stock. It'll need a gunsmith, and a forge."

He thrust the rifle roughly back at Frink wrenching the rifle from the next recruit whose hammer had clicked harmlessly.

"The whole top half of this hammer is gone."

Colburn leaned the defective rifles against a tree.

"Where's the bayonet that goes with this one?" he asked the second soldier.

"There was none given me, Sergeant."

"This is what we'll do," Colburn announced. He instructed them in marksmanship, allowing the five new recruits to share the three working Springfields. When they concluded after an hour, he marched the group back to their encampment, two of the soldiers shouldering useless weapons.

Just short of their bivouac the sergeant spotted Lieutenant William Preston. Commanding the recruits to continue to their tents the sergeant turned and walked with his lieutenant.

"And..?" the lieutenant asked when the five soldiers had moved out of earshot.

"Why can't new recruits go to camp? We mustered in Manchester in December of '61, spent eight weeks drilling there and in the White Street Barracks in New York, before coming south in February."

"We had over seventeen hundred officers and men then," the lieutenant countered. "After Wagner, Sumter, Charleston, between disease and the Confederates, we've lost over two hundred. We need replacements. Colonel Abbott thinks we can train the men here, let them mix in with the veterans; the new ones can learn."

"With what weapons?" The sergeant turned and spit into the brush. "We got a bad trade with the 40th. Half these muskets we got now aren't worthy."

"We'll have the time." Lieutenant Preston turned and resumed walking. "General Gillmore left yesterday for Hilton Head, leaving General Seymour in command. I have it from General Seymour's clerk that General Gillmore gave strict orders not to launch any offensive until he gets back. We can use these raids against the enemy's supply routes to train. We can handle the local Florida militias."

Sergeant Colburn shook his head. "Strict orders you say? Begging the lieutenant's pardon, but methinks General Seymour does suffer from the melancholia. Several of the men say so. One day they say the general can't get out of bed, and thinks himself a fool, and the next day he's running around claiming he can lick the world. You never know on any of the Lord's days what mood suits him, or which general you'll get. I had an uncle like that in Weare. They say there's no cure for the melancholia."

"I've heard those reports myself," Lieutenant Preston said. "Be that as it may, melancholia or no, General Seymour would never disobey a direct order."

CHAPTER 6

Two Days Ago

Even before I exited my BMW in the parking lot I knew that the legislative hearing was going to be different from the Parks Department show the day before. The lot was filled. I circled back and left my car on the street. People clustered around vehicles, conversing in an excited, determined fashion. Glancing at the school's front door, I experienced a momentary panic that I was too late for a seat. Most of the crowd was content to stay outside for now, and I hurried past, clutching my steno pad.

The gymnasium was alive with an energy that the Parks hearing lacked. I counted at least four full-decked Confederate officer uniforms, and a couple of others I wasn't sure about. Re-enactors always seemed to choose an officer's uniform. No one wants to portray the cannon fodder.

My seat from the day before was still empty, and as I slid into it I surveyed the room. In addition to the four full officers, several women wore period Southern dress, complete with hoops.

I studied the uniforms. One of the "officers" carried a sword belted at his hip. I checked for side arms—legal in Florida if carried openly—but saw none. I'm not sure what I would've done if I had spotted one of the colonels packing.

Two other men in civilian suits entered and began hanging a large Confederate battle flag on the back wall opposite the podium. Given the cinder block construction, I wondered how they'd attach it. They produced a variety of tape and sticky hangers, and expertly draped the St. Charles Cross. This was not the first time they'd done this.

I spotted Bill Dunleavy crammed against the far wall, two-thirds of the way back. He was bare-headed, and from his arm movements it looked like his hands were giving that Union cap a good workout. I hoped it wasn't an original.

Bill and another man flanked a woman, and I wondered whether his wife had recovered. At least today he had moral support for a hearing I figured wouldn't go well for him.

I recognized a couple of reporters from the Florida Times-Union in Jacksonville and the Miami Herald. We exchanged nods.

Agnes Thornberry had said she might attend—at least she had when I pressed her at the battlefield—but I didn't see her. No matter, she said if she wasn't there I should go to her house afterwards to learn the rest of her oral history. By the look of the crowd I suspected I might enjoy that more.

The hearing was called to order. It was announced as a public hearing of a legislative subcommittee, convened at the request of Florida State Representative Dana Chatelle, co-signer of a bill intended to remove authority from the Department of Parks to grant permission to erect monuments on Park land, and to vest said authority solely in the legislature. The bill had been referred to this subcommittee. As the bill's sponsor, Representative Chatelle would speak first, followed by anyone who wished to speak in favor. After that, anyone opposed would have a turn.

I half expected Representative Chatelle to be one of the gray uniformed soldiers, but he was a fit, early thirties man in a dark suit and conservative tie. He faced the committee members and launched into his explanation.

The bill was designed, he explained, merely to correct an error. He characterized it as a drafting oversight in the current law. The erection of monuments on state property is not, and should not be, an administrative matter. Monuments on state land represented philosophical statements and positions endorsed by the State of Florida. To whom or what a monument is dedicated is different from what type of vegetation should be planted in a given park. As such, that decision should rest not with unelected bureaucrats, but with the people themselves through their elected representatives. The Parks Department could decide which trees should be planted but should not be allowed to decide who or what to honor.

The last statement evoked a smattering of applause.

Florida's heritage, he continued, was under attack. Over one hundred and fifty years ago the citizens of Florida banded together to decide their own policies, their own way of life.

"Now," he revved up as two photographers clicked away, "some of those decisions may not have been the best, but the enduring principle was that Floridians should decide the policies and laws of Florida. To oppose the efforts of those in other states to dictate what Florida's policies should be, brave Floridians answered the call of their governor to resist this invasion by Northern states.

"A great battle was fought at Olustee, near Ocean Pond," he continued, "a battle as important to the citizens of Florida as the Battle of Hastings was to the Anglo-Saxon people of Britain in 1066." It was, he argued, a resistance to a foreign force.

I gave up writing verbatim and began summarizing to keep up. I cursed myself for not bringing a digital recorder.

To honor its citizens who had fought so bravely, he argued, the State of Florida had erected three monuments on Florida state land. Whether the State of Florida would, or should, erect a monument on state land honoring those who had come to invade Florida and kill Floridians, was a policy decision that needed to be made by Florida's citizens through their elected representatives, not by administrative bureaucrats based on the size or weight of the monument.

"A Union monument to federal soldiers might indeed be appropriate," he concluded as a camera flashed, "but only if erected on *federal* land."

More applause followed his speech.

Next up was one of the gray uniformed officers who identified himself as a member of the Sons of Confederate Veterans. He talked about the growing attacks across the country to besmirch Southern heritage, to make everyone think that the brave soldiers who had answered their state's call to service were nothing more than slavers and racists. He mentioned the events of Charleston, and the shame and embarrassment he felt as he watched on Fox

News the honorable battle flag across from the South Carolina Statehouse lowered for the last time.

"Florida was united in spirit in 1864," he said. "Now, people who aren't even from Florida want to come down here and tell us what we should do with our land, the very land our citizens shed blood to protect."

At about the fourth speaker I started thinking maybe I should be writing a piece on the on-going attack on Southern heritage. The major outlets had obviously missed this story. Pulitzer stuff here, no doubt.

But the cake was when another uniformed guy got up and started in on the same theme. "This is our state," he finished, standing and raising his arms. "*This*, is Dixie."

With that he turned and faced the crowd. I don't know if the whole thing was orchestrated, but several audience members, including one of the hoop-skirted belles, stood and broke into a rendition of the song "Dixie." The tune gathered momentum, and soon most of the room was standing, swaying and singing. I can't say what the reaction was of the legislators behind their table, because I too had grabbed my camera and was clicking away. I got up and moved to the front—decorum be damned—I wanted a picture with the Confederate flag draped behind the singers.

Eventually Bill Dunleavy got up and spoke in opposition to the bill, but it was more to support the monument than to argue against the legislative policy issue Chatelle was pushing.

When the hearing ended I hurried to my car. I could call Dunleavy later. I wanted to get to Agnes Thornberry's house and learn the rest of the story about her great-grandmother. It was fourteen minutes from the school to her house. As I pulled into her driveway she was placing two bags of groceries on her front stoop.

"Come on in," she called over her shoulder as I exited my car. She unlocked the front door and entered her cottage. I scooped up the bags and followed her.

"Just put them on the table," she instructed, removing her jacket and disappearing into her bedroom. "I'll put them away later. Nothing perishable."

When she returned, she had changed into a light sweater.

"I don't buy nearly as much food since Albert died." She peered into the grocery bags.

She must have sensed my reaction because she almost smiled when she looked up.

"Passing is something you do in football. My husband of forty-three years died, and I say it plain. It doesn't make it easier to say one word or the other.

"When you go to the grocery store today it's hard to imagine how difficult it was to get fresh vegetables back then." She indicated a chair for me to sit on. "Hard drive by team from farm to your market, and then the even rockier drive back with the lurching wagon afterwards…"

CHAPTER 7

Jacksonville-Lake City Road
Tuesday, February 16, 1864

Frederick Mallory eased his grip and let the reins slip through his hands to allow the team to set their own pace. The pair of horses surged, as if aware that they were heading back toward their farm and stable. They pulled harder than they had on the way to Jacksonville. But the wagon was lighter now.

Miriam Aggafor squirmed from the constant jouncing. She'd arch up off the seat to avoid a severe jolt. The road was rough, a narrow, stony strip twisting between thick pine on both sides.

Mallory smiled. "It'll only be three hours, ma'am."

Miriam sighed and readjusted the empty sacks she had placed under herself on the wooden slat of a bench.

"A saddle is so much more comfortable." She raised her arm to block a tree branch. It swung past her hand anyway and lashed her face.

"But you can't move goods to market on horseback." He flicked the reins as the horses struggled across a shallow depression filled with rainwater. The wheels stuck momentarily. Mallory feared he'd have to dismount and tug the wagon through the muck. But the horses strained free.

"It was better going there," she said. "The weight of the load kept the wagon steadier."

Mallory nodded. "It could have been worse. By setting up camp this far west of Jacksonville, the federals cut our trip from two days each way to a half day."

He watched her head snap back as a deep rut jolted the wagon.

She nodded at his hands. "You drive a lot in the army?"

He stared straight ahead as the wagon lurched over a rock.

"I mostly rode."

"Cavalry?"

He nodded. "Grew up with horses. Trained them, rode them. Shot from them."

"Until you got tired of killing from them?"

"Something like that."

The road veered left, and the wagon climbed over the railroad bed. The road swung right again, and the wagon continued west, now on the south side of the tracks.

"That line get much use?" Mallory asked.

"Not since the war come. It was finished just 'afore the war started. Connected the east coast to the Gulf. Was supposed to carry all kinds of goods from Jacksonville to over Gulf way.

"My daddy always wanted a railroad alongside our property. Said we could ship crops to market. Mr. Yulee started it nine years ago. But the war come, and the Yankees captured Jacksonville. It ain't run much since.

"Then daddy died of the fever. That rail line's been rotting away, what with the Yankees holding both ends."

"Your daddy sick long?"

"Not much. He cut himself on a fence post and came down with a fever. Since he died mama hardly leaves her room. That and Johnny getting himself killed.

"Were you there?" she asked suddenly, twisting to look at the wagon's driver. "It was in Georgia."

Frederick Mallory shook his head. "No, ma'am."

Miriam turned back forward. "I heard Chickamauga was just a swamp in the woods, all vines and bugs.

"Just like this road." She swatted at a mosquito. "You get bugs this big up where you're from?"

"Not hardly."

"It's not even dark out. You know, I never did hear how Johnny died. What happened, I mean."

"Sometimes it's best not to know."

"You think so?" She turned to him again. "Truly?"

"All that matters is that he did what he thought he ought to do, and now he's gone. Remember him as you knew him growing up, when you were happy children."

"He weren't happy, long before he was killed. He should have done what you did and run away. No offense intended," she added quickly.

"None taken."

"Let me ask you plain. If you don't care anymore about the war, or the Confederacy, or whatever it was made you run, how come you didn't take a job back there for the Yankees? They pay in gold."

"I don't know. Maybe once I got there it didn't seem right."

"I don't know about that. They said deserters worked for them. Scouts and what not. And some still wore the gray. The way I hear it, their General Seymour has some big orders from Lincoln himself to be fair to everyone, and hire even former Confederate soldiers if they take an oath."

"Once I got there, I just couldn't do it," he repeated. "It didn't seem right."

"I can't keep you on at the farm. I don't have money to pay you. Lest that was what you were thinking."

"I know that."

"Although I could use the help. Before the war there was Papa, and Johnny when he got older. We even had a field hand, but he run off as soon as the Yankees took Jacksonville."

"And joined the Federal Navy."

"How's you know that…? Oh, Hanna," she guessed. "I think she's proud of him. Thinks he's gonna' come sailing up the St. Mary River in some big old Yankee gunboat and take her away too." Miriam chuckled. "That's her dream."

"Was that her man?"

"Goodness, no. She's my uncle's house servant. Uncle Jacob brought her over when he joined up, him not being married and having no children. He just brought her over, left her off, and up and joined the Army. His farm's been growing over these past two years. At first Papa farmed it a bit with Johnny and the field hand, but then…"

"I know." Mallory looked at her earnestly. "Look, I just need a place to stay while I figure out what to do. A roof over my head and some food. Regular food. Why don't I stay on for a few days? You already have another full wagon you could sell. And now that we know the Yankees are only a half day away, and we don't have to go all the way to Jacksonville, why, I could drive in and back in one day next time. I could go back tomorrow or the day after."

"How do I know you'll come back with my wagon, or my horses, or my money?"

Mallory laughed. "That's easy. Come with me."

CHAPTER 8

8th Regiment, United States Colored Troops
Encampment, Barber Plantation
West of Jacksonville
Thursday, February 18, 1864
Evening

"I think we be going soon," Corporal Thomas Cotton announced as he approached the tent.

"Back to Jacksonville?" Charles Dunhill craned his head outside. He reached one hand out, palm up. When it remained dry he scrambled out of the tent.

The corporal shook his head. "We be marching. West. Along the rail line to the reb camp in Lake City. The big one."

Private Jeffers lay sprawled outside the tent, whittling. He looked up. "How can that be?"

"It can't be true." Charles hitched his pants. "Who said that? Orders from the lieutenant?"

Thomas Cotton shook his head. "I heard it from the men over at the New Hampshire 7th."

Jeffers scoffed and resumed carving. "Them white boys messing with you. Trying to get you all rattled up. Think it's fun trying to scare us. Just because they've been in scraps already."

"No, I think it's the Lord's truth."

Private Jeffers pointed the carving knife at his corporal. "Two days ago you telling us how them New Hampshire boys be saying that General Gillmore sailed back up to Hilton Head, and told General Seymour he weren't to take no action no how against anyone 'til the good general himself returned. You saying the good general changed his mind and sent some note back on a boat coming this-a-way?"

Corporal Cotton shook his head. "That's not it. Them New Hampshire boys told me General Seymour's clerk, he took a letter for the general yesterday and sent it up after General Gillmore by steamer. Letter will catch up with General Gillmore in Hilton Head. It says that General Seymour is going to attack with full force against the rebs in Lake City, and then capture the rail line at the Suwanee River."

Jeffers let out a low whistle. "Iffin' General Gillmore left General Seymour in charge with orders not to attack, and General Seymour waited until General Gillmore was gone, and then sent that letter, why General Seymour is going to be in a world of whipping when General Gillmore gets back."

"We be going soon, then," Corporal Cotton said.

"Them New Hampshire boys tell you that? They know when we're going?"

"No, but if General Seymour chase General Gillmore with a letter, he's got to know that Gillmore, he gonna' send a letter right back down here ordering General Seymour to sit and wait. We gonna' be moving out 'afore it gets here."

"Lordy, if what you say be true, we might be marching soon."

Private Jeffers punched Charles in the arm. "Looks like it finally makes sense, you coming down here from Pennsylvania and all. And me from Indiana, together we're going to finally whip them rebs."

"Now if we could just whip them all to Virginia, I might get to see my mother again." Corporal Cotton smiled.

"How'd y'all get to Pennsylvania anyway?" Jeffers asked. "I mean, most of this regiment is free blacks from Pennsylvania and Indiana, but how'd you join this one?"

Corporal Cotton dropped to the ground next to Jeffers and removed his shoes, stretching his feet to the fire.

"I was always looking. Every day I thought about it. If a white man passed through and was talking about where he'd been and what he'd seen, I always listened. When the war come and a lot of the whites went off to fight, we thought we'd have a better chance then, but after that they watched closer. The plantation was only a few miles from the Maryland border, and two summers ago I found my chance. Stonewall Jackson backed out of the Shenandoah spring before last. In the confusion hundreds of us ran through the lines to freedom. I worked my way north and ended up in Pittsburgh that fall.

"Then last September I heard they were forming a colored regiment and I knew right off I wanted to join. They began taking us in November, and I was there the first day."

"My own mother escaped twenty-five years ago," Charles said. "A few of them got smuggled up by white abolitionists and settled in Pennsylvania. Worked on an abolitionist farm near the Maryland border. That's where she met my father. He be white. My brother and I were born free, but we did what we could to help other runaways. Thought we had a pretty good life."

"Until last summer," Charles added. "It all changed then."

The group around the campfire grew quiet.

Charles Dunhill tossed another twig on the fire and watched it flare.

"Last summer, when Lee come across the border from Maryland with his seventy thousand reb army, he came right past Mr. Sennett's farm. We had a warning rebs was a-coming. I thought we had nothing to fear—we was free—but my parents were scared, and Mr. Sennett, he said you can't trust them. He made us go in a wagon to his sister's in Harrisburg. Just leave, take nothing, just go. Hid in the back of a wagon with sacks over us in the June sun we did, all the way to Harrisburg."

"You all make it safe?" Corporal Cotton asked.

Charles nodded. "We did. And stayed with Mr. Sennett's sister and her husband in Harrisburg for two weeks, until after we was sure the rebs were across the river and back in Virginia. Then we headed back to the Sennett farm since there was still a whole summer crop that was coming in, and me and my father felt obliged."

The fire crackled. No one spoke, or pressed Charles Dunhill to finish his story. The private took a deep breath.

"We didn't know what might happen to Mr. Sennett, being he had helped so many escape, but they left him alone. Killed his cattle for beef, but let him and his family be. But they took my brother."

"Took him?" a soldier asked.

Charles nodded. "The rebs grabbed every black they found in Pennsylvania. Either killed them on the spot as an escaped slave or took them prisoner as an escaped slave. Brought them back to Virginia to be sold. They took Benjamin."

"He didn't go to Harrisburg with you?"

Charles Dunhill shook his head. "He was out hunting. We only had an hour or two warning. Mr. Sennett put every black on his farm in that wagon and had my father drive it as fast as he could. Mr. Sennett said he'd find Benjamin and hide him. But when Benjamin come back, the rebs were already at the farm. Mr. Sennett tried to tell them that Benjamin was born free, but they just struck him to the ground and took him. Some reb claimed he recognized him as a runaway. It didn't matter, they took everyone, least ways the ones that didn't resist and got themselves killed. And like me, Benjamin is light skinned. That made the rebs even more angry."

"And you haven't heard?" Jeffers asked.

Charles spit into the fire. "Maybe if this war goes long enough and I fight long enough, I'll find him. Like all of you, I joined the 8th as soon as I could. But Benjamin, he never was a slave. I fear he won't do well."

CHAPTER 9

Samuels-Aggafor Farm
Sanderson, Florida
Thursday, February 18, 1864
Evening

Hanna placed the tray with the evening meal on the table next to Eleanor Aggafor's bed.

"You want help to sit up, ma'am?"

The woman opened her eyes and squinted. "Why, why, you're back."

"I brought you breakfast this morning, missus. I thought you was asleep so I left it."

Eleanor Aggafor pushed up on her pillows and blinked. She stared hard.

"You're not him. You're that slave. I thought you was Johnny."

"No, ma'am." Hanna bent over and gently tugged on the worn housecoat until the lady sat fully upright. Once she got her situated Hanna reached for the tray.

"Leave it," the old lady commanded with a wave of her hand.

She stared hard as Hanna straightened the bedclothes.

"There's no lamp lit. In the dim light…"

"Yes, ma'am." Hanna knew better than to comment.

It was not the first time that Miriam Aggafor's mother had stared at her. And not the first time she had called her Johnny. The lady's mind was failing as fast as her eyes.

Hanna hadn't minded at first. But after word reached the farm the previous fall that Johnny Aggafor had been killed, Hanna shuddered every time the old lady repeated her delusional observation.

In her years of enslavement to Eleanor's brother, Jacob Samuels, on the adjacent farm, the old lady had never paid her much heed. But of course, the old lady's husband was alive then, and she was still in her right mind.

A noise from the hall made her turn.

"Mother." Miriam Aggafor bustled into the room. "You haven't eaten all day. The doctor says you must."

"I've eaten enough all these years."

Moving to the window, Hanna pulled in the shutters. If the whites wanted her to do something different they'd tell her.

"I'll have my own dinner downstairs, Hanna," Miriam said.

"Yes, ma'am."

"You went down and back to Jacksonville already." The old lady studied her daughter. "Lessen' you took a train, and there ain't been none these two years."

Perhaps the old lady was not as insane as she sometimes acted, Hanna reasoned as she gathered soiled laundry off the floor.

"We didn't go all the way to Jacksonville, Mama. Most of the Yankees moved out to the old Barber Plantation. With a dry road we got there in less than half a day. There and back in less than a day if we chose."

"So you sold our food to the Yankees?" The old lady scowled. "The ones that killed Johnny?"

If the elder white woman was confused when she first awoke, she seemed to be getting a clear head now.

"I took Yankee gold from them that killed Johnny." Miriam sat on the edge of the bed. "Figured it was part of what they owed us."

"Leave that!" the old lady commanded, turning to the slave. "That's not dirty. I need it against the night air."

"Yes, ma'am." Hanna refolded the cloak, covering the food stain, and draped the garment across the back of the wicker rocker in the corner.

"What about that man that's been about the farm these last few days?" the old lady asked. "Uniform? Confederate soldier?"

"Deserter."

"Well, where's he at? I ain't seen no other man 'round here, at least, not since war come."

"He's gone." Miriam smoothed the edges of the quilt.

"Gone where?" Eleanor demanded.

Miriam shrugged. "Gone where all deserters go. Deep woods, or maybe further south where no one's at. He talked about working for the Yankees in Jacksonville. He could ride some, leastways, he knew his way around horses. I figure he'll either scout for the Yankees, or maybe hitch on as a cracker with one of them cattle drives to the Georgia rail yards. He said he was from Georgia, if you can believe a deserter."

"We could have used him."

"Now Mama, we don't have money to be hiring help."

"You got that gold from peddling to the Yankees," Eleanor retorted. "You don't seem to mind about that. And we could use a man around here, what with Pa and Johnny both gone to the Lord.

"And my brother, Jacob? We still haven't heard any word from him?"

Miriam shook her head.

"Help me up," her mother said. Miriam stood up off the bed and backed away as Eleanor swung her feet to the floor.

"I think I'll set a spell. If you get me a candle I might read a verse or two."

Hanna rushed to the bed, and together with Miriam helped the old woman stand. Each holding an arm, they assisted as she shuffled across the room to the wicker rocker. Hanna steadied the woman with one hand and swept up the folded cloak with the other.

"You want a pillow, ma'am?" Hanna asked after settling the woman onto the rocker.

Eleanor didn't answer. Hanna carried the soiled cloak into the hall.

"It wouldn't hurt to have a man about," Eleanor repeated to her daughter. "Jacob's land just sits there, fields untilled, us supporting his slave. Should just sell her for whatever we can get. I say do it now before the Yankees come and she runs off and we get nothing for her. Maybe sell her the next time the crackers drive through. They could get good money for her in Georgia, and they always have money in their pockets to pay."

Miriam tilted her head to the side.

"It's a good idea, but I don't think we should be selling any of Jacob's property without his permission. He'll raise Cain with us when he comes back if we sold his slave."

"*If* he comes back," Eleanor corrected. "He should have made some provision for us having to provide food to her while he's away. Of course, he never thought of that before he up and joined the fight. Too old to go, I told him, even if he is fifteen years younger than me. And now we got no word."

"I think I will have a bite." The old woman scanned the room. Her eyes settled on the dinner plate. "Where'd that dang girl get to?"

Hanna stepped back into the room and moved to the bedside table. She carried the plate to a table near the rocker.

"And what about you?" Eleanor turned her focus on her daughter. "Having a man around here, why, there haven't been any living around here since war come. The Dobson boys, Harold Raftery's son, they all gone off. No one left for you now, is there?" She cackled.

"Now, Mama," Miriam protested.

"I'm serious, child. What with this here war who's left for you to marry? This farm needs a man. I always thought it'd be Johnny. Maybe that's why you sell in Jacksonville. Figure you'll find yourself a Yankee."

CHAPTER 10

General Alfred Colquitt raised his eyebrows when he spotted the lanky soldier in disheveled grays ambling up the incline toward his tent. He frowned at the tattered sleeves where the soldier's rank should have been. He waved him forward, turned and led the way under the flap. He dismissed his orderly and gestured for the man to sit. The orderly withdrew.

"I thought you were going to join the Union Army," the general said. A solitary wooden plank lay propped across two camp stools. A map lay across the makeshift table, its edges draping to the ground. General Colquitt moved to the far side and sat, pointing at a fourth stool.

"I couldn't, sir." Captain Frederick Mallory positioned his frame opposite the general.

"Wouldn't let you, eh? I thought Gillmore and Seymour were following Lincoln's latest directive and welcoming all Southerners and Confederate fighters back into their fold. I figured you'd be gone for weeks."

"It wasn't that, sir. I could have gotten a job as a scout. As you say, I would not have been the first."

The general's eyes narrowed. "That was the plan, Captain. Why didn't you follow it?"

The captain hesitated. "They . . . there was a requirement that to work for them you had to take an oath. I wouldn't do it."

The general studied his cavalry captain.

"Even though it wouldn't have been a real oath in your heart, Captain?"

"Because it would not have been a real oath in my heart. Sir."

The general nodded solemnly. Abruptly standing, he retreated to the back of the tent, returning with a bottle of bourbon.

"Drink?"

The captain waved him off. "In any event, it didn't matter. I got lucky."

"God shines fortune on those who deserve." The general poured a glass for himself.

"And sometimes people just get lucky."

"Still," the general said, between sips. "You've only been gone six days. Hardly enough time to make it to Jacksonville, observe and return."

The captain nodded. "I reached a farm about ten miles due east of here. It's run by a young woman."

When the general raised his eyebrows the captain quickly explained.

"Her father's dead and her only brother was killed last year. She has an uncle, but he's serving up north. It's just her, an invalid mother and a darkie house servant who works in the field."

"It doesn't sound like a successful enterprise."

"It's not. She sells what she can in Jacksonville. I offered to help her bring a wagon load there, figuring I might attract less suspicion riding in with her. Would have been a two-day trip—maybe forty miles one way."

The general nodded.

Captain Mallory reached over and tugged at the map that stretched across the make-shift table. He ran his fingers over the folds and jabbed at a spot. The general leaned forward.

"We only got about twelve miles," the captain explained. "Reached Barber Plantation, just about dead on between Sanderson and Jacksonville. Maybe 35 miles east of Lake City. They've got about six thousand men there under General Truman Seymour. They've got the 7th New Hampshire, or what's left of it. Abbot's regiment. A veteran bunch, but shot up pretty bad. Also the 8th Colored, pretty much full strength. They say they formed up in Pennsylvania last fall, and just arrived down here.

Made up of free blacks from Pennsylvania and Indiana, but no battle experience. Two companies of the 54th Massachusetts, the colored outfit that charged Fort Wagner last summer; that's a pretty veteran outfit. The North Carolina First Colored too, made up of escaped slaves from the Carolinas. Again, no experience. And then there's the 7th Connecticut. They've been given Spencer repeating rifles. Barton's New Yorkers. Maybe six thousand in all."

The general nodded. "And you found all this out while selling vegetables? In one trip?"

The captain shook his head. "No, sir. I headed off three days ago. Figured it would take two days to do the forty miles to Jacksonville. Like I say, I had a bit of good fortune. A half day east of Sanderson by wagon we run into the whole Union force camped at that plantation. Made it back to the farm the next day, then made a second trip to the plantation early this morning. The federals been using the plantation as a camp. In addition to the infantry there's some field pieces, Henry's Massachusetts Cavalry. They've been raiding against local militia, grabbing supplies, some beef."

"They skirmished outside of Lake City seven days ago," the general said. "But from your description it sounds more like a field hospital than a camp. Untested regiment, a shot-up New Hampshire 7th, new nigger outfits. I doubt they'll move. General Beauregard may have sent us down here for nothing."

"When did you arrive, General?"

"Today." Colquitt studied the map in greater detail.

"Do you think this Barber position can be taken, since I don't think they're going anywhere?"

Captain Mallory shook his head vigorously. "The ground between here and there is terrible. All swamp and pine. There's no open fields on which either side could move. What farms there are along the way are too small to maneuver over. Any fighting would be in the woods. There's a wagon track that runs east from here to Jacksonville, and both sides would have to use it to approach the other. It's narrow, no more than four men could march abreast. It runs close to the rail line, which is just five-foot gauge, with not much clearing on either side. The locals say that tree branches swipe at passing trains, engineers keep their heads inside, that's how narrow the cleared line is. And not much has run on that line in almost two years, so it hasn't gotten wider. Still, it could be used to march."

"I doubt it," the general mused. "No army could maneuver in the country you've just described."

Captain Mallory frowned. "I would have thought so, too. When I got to their encampment three days ago their soldiers were saying that General Gillmore had left that day for consultations at Hilton Head, and left strict orders for General Seymour not to advance. Apparently General Gillmore appreciates the situation. The federals thought they might have a few more days of raiding, and then march back to Jacksonville for the rest of the winter."

"And?"

"Well, sir, when I was there today everything was different. Rumors were everywhere that General Seymour sent a letter to General Gillmore in Hilton Head just yesterday saying he was going to advance on the rail bridge at the Suwanee River, which is well west of Lake City."

Mallory jabbed at the map. "The federals think it's only General Finnigan and his Florida militia at Lake City, so Seymour probably figures he can overrun them easily. They don't know we were sent down here, sir."

"And they told you all this? You think it reliable?"

Mallory straightened up "Sir, this is like no military camp I've ever seen. Little security. Civilians strolling everywhere. Soldiers talking freely about their units. Confederate deserters walking about, working as laborers and scouts. So yes, I think it's reliable."

"You say General Seymour sent that letter up yesterday?"

"Heard it from soldiers in two separate Union regiments."

General Colquitt tugged the map toward himself. He traced several lines with his fingers running west from Jacksonville.

"So, when the cat's away, the mouse will play, eh? If this is all true, Captain, Seymour will move before Gillmore returns or relieves him of command. Within the next two days, three at most. He may move tomorrow, or perhaps Saturday."

The general pointed down at the map. "With the terrain as you say, neither side can mount much of an attack. This calls for a defensive strategy. Seymour will advance in columns along the road or the rail bed, intent on marching all the way to Lake City.

"We're setting up good earthen fortifications here. We've chosen this place carefully. There's all swamp and thick pines to the south, and a lake—" Colquitt jabbed at the map again "—here, just to the north of us."

The general leaned in closer. "It's called Ocean Pond. By moving ten miles east from Lake City we've reached a point where the passable terrain is narrow. If we can get them to attack us here—" the general again jabbed at the map "—we can lead them into the cauldron. The terrain will make it impossible to flank us. You think the pine where you scouted is thick enough to mask our position?"

"Definitely."

"Excellent. We'll put your 4th Georgia Cavalry to the north, Captain. To fend off the Yankee cavalry. We need to prepare to move.

"Orderly!" the general barked.

"Request that I be allowed to meet with General Finnigan immediately," the general said when the orderly appeared.

CHAPTER 11

8th Regiment, United States Colored Troops
Barber Plantation
28 miles west of Jacksonville
12 miles east of Sanderson
Friday, February 19, 1864
Evening

"We're heading out tomorrow," Corporal Cotton announced.

Private Charles Dunhill did not believe it. "Who says?"

Lowering the butt of his Springfield to the ground, the corporal leaned the rifle against a tree. He approached the campfire

"Everyone says so. But Lieutenant Norton, he told us direct."

"Back to Jacksonville? We done here?" Private Latoya asked.

Squatting on his haunches, the corporal extended his hands over the dying embers.

"Not Jacksonville. We're marching on Lake City."

Charles Dunhill let out a soft whistle. "You sure?"

"Of course I'm sure. Like I said, Lieutenant Norton told me direct, and white officers aren't allowed to lie or make stuff up."

"Well, seeing how all officers are white that would mean officers always tell the truth, and we know that ain't so."

There was grumbled laughter from around the campfire.

"Well, it's still true," Corporal Cotton insisted. "The lieutenant told me to pass the word along, and that's what I'm doing. He said it's all planned. General Seymour will lead us."

"We all going?" a soldier from back in the shadows asked.

"Not all. Abbott's New Hampshire boys be marching in the lead, then the Connecticut 7th, then us. They're going to leave the 54th Massachusetts and the North Carolina First Colored back to guard the rail line and supplies and then follow behind."

"How many?" Charles asked.

"The lieutenant says we'll have about five thousand altogether," Corporal Cotton responded. "We'll set off at daybreak, and the general wants to cover at least fifteen, maybe twenty miles tomorrow. We'll camp just outside of Lake City and attack the rebs Sunday morning."

Charles Dunhill cleared his throat. "How many rebs?"

The corporal shrugged. "Our scouts say they're camped at Lake City all winter. Maybe two thousand. But they're all Florida militia. Once we rout them, the whole path to the Gulf'll be open."

The group let out muffled approval.

"And Georgia," the soldier in the shadows said. "If we beat those rebs over at Lake City, why, the whole bottom of Georgia be wide open."

There was more muffled assent.

"You're all crazy," Charles said. "We can't take Georgia with five thousand men."

"There ain't never been five thousand like us," another soldier chimed in to more laughter.

"I gotta' take a pee." Charles stood up. He headed toward the latrines at the edge of the clearing. As he undid his pants, he heard rustling behind him. He turned.

Corporal Cotton stood in the moonlight. "You not sounding like you ready to fight. The men are going to take that from you. Isn't this what we signed up for?"

Private Dunhill spit into the bushes. "It be what we signed up for, me, you, every man here, but I dunno'."

"'Bout what?"

Dunhill took a deep breath. Behind the corporal the talk grew louder around the campfires, and there was more laughter than usual. It's forced, he thought. They're scared.

"If you be scared, the men will sense that," Corporal Cotton said, as if reading the private's thoughts. "I was a slave. Now I'm a corporal, but you born free, and can read and write. The men respect you. I don't know why Colonel Fribley made me a corporal and not you."

"Yeah, of course I'm scared." Charles pointed back at the fires. "The men are scared too, but there's no shame in that. We all signed up knowing we could die, but thinking it be worth it. But that's not why I'm thinking the way I am."

"Then what is it?"

"We ain't trained proper. We all joined up in Pennsylvania last November. We trained two months before heading to New York, trained a bit there, then came to Hilton Head and then down here. But we never been in shooting, never heard no shots fired at us."

"But we trained," the corporal pressed. "No one's ever been in a fight 'til they been in one."

Charles Dunhill shook his head. "At camp they tell us we got to be able to load and fire three times in one minute. But standing in a line, rebs shooting at us, how many of the men could do that? And Colonel Fribley, he tried to get us more time to practice loading and shooting, but every time he asked he was told there wasn't enough powder and shot to practice. So all we be doing for three months is marching and parading. And now, tomorrow, we going to march across land we don't know, and then attack rebs in their state, never having fought before?"

"You've had too much book-learning," Corporal Cotton said. "General Seymour and Colonel Fribley know all that, that's why they're puttin' us at the back of Hawley's Brigade. Them New Hampshire boys be in front, and they was with the 54th at Fort Wagner."

"That's another thing," Charles argued. "Yeah, the New Hampshire 7th is experienced, but they be shot up pretty good right now. I been talking to some of them white Abbott's boys. Their whole regiment is filled with replacements. I heard some of them don't even speak no English."

"But they got veterans to show them the way."

"Sure they do." The private finished and hitched his pants back up. He turned to the corporal. "Good ones too. But half their rifles are missing pieces, and hardly any have bayonets."

Corporal Cotton shook his head. "Charles, it's militia. The men see you worrying too much they'll get scared. We'll be fine at Lake City. Remember, we got the Lord on our side."

Greg Ahlgren

Confederate Camp Beauregard
West of Sanderson
Friday, February 19, 1864
Evening

Captain Frederick Mallory walked toward the improvised corral at Camp Beauregard. From all corners the sounds of preparation reached him. Axes rang against tree trunks, pine branches crashed to the ground, and hoes dug into the soft clay to shovel soil in between layered timbers. If the Yankees didn't arrive the next day, they would be here by Sunday at the latest, and Mallory knew his Confederates would be ready.

The captain found his mount and saddle, and as he did on the eve of each battle, checked and rechecked the leather. Ten feet away, a young private he didn't recognize in the darkness checked his own mount.

"Where you from?" Mallory hoped it sounded friendly.

"Georgia, sir. The Fourth Georgia Cavalry." When the private looked up, he studied Mallory's re-sewn insignia. The private squinted before drawing himself to full attention.

"I'm sorry, sir. I didn't recognize you, Captain."

"Long ways." Mallory stroked the withers of his horse.

The private's voice was familiar. He strained in the dim light, trying to place a name with the voice. The stallion nuzzled Mallory's hand.

"Captain, I thought you had deserted. Well, not deserted," the private stammered. "I mean, I didn't think that, I know you wouldn't, but that's what some said. No one would say why you left. Not even the officers. Then today someone said you was back. Our whole unit done come down from Georgia. The day before General Colquitt and General Harrison arrived with their own infantry brigades."

Mallory nodded. "We're putting together a strong enough force to counter the Yankees, if they come.

"Penniman, isn't it?" Mallory suddenly remembered. "Private William Pennimen?"

"Yes, sir!" The private beamed.

"Oh, they'll come all right," Penniman added. "The whole lot of them. Colonel Clinch told us that an army of thirty thousand Yankee niggers is going to be marching on Lake City, and we needed to get down here to save the city, and all Florida."

"Thirty thousand niggers, he said? Duncan Clinch said that?"

"Yes, sir. That's what he told us. Why, we rode down here in a forced march. Kept trotting the horses at the quick when we could. No provisions, just bedding on our saddles, no food wagon, nothing. Nothing for my horse except water when we come across a clear stream.

"Poor horse is half-starved." The private turned and patted his mount. "But we got here in time. We got two hundred fifty here from the Georgia 4th Cavalry. And there be another two hundred in the Florida 2nd Cavalry under Colonel McCormick. General Smith is in charge of both cavalries.

"We got to see General Colquitt and General Harrison arrive with their own brigades. Them boys look powerful young, but they already been in many a battle."

From the surrounding pine the sound of banjos and singing reached the corral as the men wound down their work of preparing fortifications and turned their attention to food and music. Mallory recognized the opening verse to the "Tenting Tonight" song that had recently begun sweeping Confederate campsites. Written by a northerner, he knew it was just as popular in their camps. The two silently listened to the harmony wafting through the trees.

Many are the hearts that are weary tonight,
Wishing for the war to cease;
Many are the hearts looking for the right
To see the dawn of peace.

"Sounds good, don't it, Captain? I mean, knowing we're all here, all in this together to save Florida. I'm told we have maybe four thousand six hundred men altogether. Just waiting for the Yankees to attack."

"Get some rest, Private." Mallory turned to leave. "And get some food for your horse. Tomorrow could be a long day."

CHAPTER 12

One Day Ago
Noon

Bill Dunleavy answered his front door on the third knock.

"Sorry," he explained sheepishly, before turning and leading me inside. "I was in the can."

His wife must have been over the flu because she joined us in the living room. Either that or she was damn insensitive to my health.

"Don't worry. I'm not contagious. Soda, Mr. Bauman?" She disappeared into the kitchen.

"Diet Coke if you've got it," I called after her, craning my neck around the door frame. "And please, call me Jason."

"I appreciate you seeing me." I turned back to Bill.

My host chuckled. "Answering Civil War questions is something I enjoy in retirement. Being a member of the Sons of Union Veterans of The Civil War is a sure sign I'm a buff."

It gave me an opening. "At the hearing two days ago you mentioned guiding visitors around whose ancestors fought here. How often does that happen?"

Bill Dunleavy considered. "Four, five times a year. Not as often as descendants of the Confederate soldiers who fought here show up. Maybe that's because those folks have a shorter distance to go. Most of the Confederates who fought here probably grew up within a hundred miles, two at most. Mostly Georgians. The Union soldiers, heck, they came here from all over the Northeast. Assuming their children and grandchildren didn't wander too far, well, the southern descendants have a geographic advantage in visiting.

"You know, interest in the war varies," he said. "After that Ken Burns series a while back, there was a definite increase, but then it died down again."

I pulled out my notebook and retrieved a pen.

"How do they find you?" I yanked off the cap with my teeth.

"The descendants? Well, if they're members of the Sons, or some other Union group, they'll get my name that way, and usually call or e-mail beforehand. Of course, some just show up without calling first. I run into them out there."

"At the battlefield? How often do you go out?"

Bill Dunleavy looked up as his wife entered with a tray.

"My wife thinks too often."

"I do not!" she chided, and they both laughed. She placed the tray on the coffee table in front of me. In addition to glasses with ice and open Diet Coke cans, there were finger sandwiches and peanuts. Even getting over the flu, Alice Dunleavy had prepared for my visit.

"I take visitors out maybe four or five times a year," Bill said. "And I go out by myself, or with Alice, on anniversaries: the battle itself on February 20 each year, and of course on Memorial Day. The real one that is, May 30, not the last Monday-of-May-beginning-of-summer-barbecue-day."

I nodded and scribbled.

"Sometimes I plant flowers," he added.

"I saw someone doing that the other day," I said. "An elderly lady."

The Dunleavys exchanged knowing looks.

"Agnes Thornberry?" Bill asked. "The Grand Lady of Olustee? I see her there a lot. I've talked to her a fair amount too."

"I met her at her home yesterday. She started telling me about her family."

"Well, she has the connection for sure. Her great-grandmother lived here during the war."

"It goes back farther than that," Alice corrected. "I think it was *her* father who owned the farm, but left it to her when he died. Isn't that right, Bill?"

"That's right. She farmed it herself for years, got married, and her kids worked it. Or at least one of them. That would be Agnes' grandmother."

"You know where the farm was?"

Bill scratched his chin and frowned. "That's a problem. I don't know where anything is anymore. The road the soldiers marched along ran past the family farm. The Union troops stopped in Sanderson and rested, ate lunch from their rations that day. But this whole area was different by the nineteen fifties. What with all the construction here after the war—"

"—that would be World War Two," Alice interjected.

"—all of northern Florida got drive-in movies and strip malls and what not. Then that new shopping center, condos, so no, I'm not sure where anything happened exactly."

"Except for the state park, which is surrounded by the national park," Alice said.

"But even there," Bill countered, "it all happened in the woods. It's not like Gettysburg where you can stand at the wall, or crawl all over the Devil's Den, or the cross-roads, where everything is marked and preserved."

"We watch that movie every year," Alice added.

"I'm sure someone could start tracing deeds." Bill shrugged. "But I'm not sure what you'd use for ground reference."

"She didn't have any brothers who fought here, right?" I asked. "Agnes has been telling me the story and I need to get more. It's only that her great grandmother lived here during that time?"

"That's something by itself. Agnes tries to keep the memory alive."

I flipped over a page and kept scribbling.

"Since you're a Sons of Union Veterans member that means your own ancestor fought in the War, but not here?"

"Not here. He was in the 34th Massachusetts Infantry. He was wounded twice, once in the Battle of New Market in the Shenandoah Valley on May 15, 1864, and then again charging Fort Gregg on the outskirts of Richmond almost a year later. The day before Richmond fell. Once Fort Gregg fell Richmond was indefensible and Lee abandoned the city. Six days later he surrendered at Appomattox."

I flipped a page.

"I've often wondered about my own great-grandfather," Bill mused. "How many guys you think were wounded twice in the Civil War and survived? Can't be many."

"But he survived?" I flipped another one.

"He did. He bought the farm all right." Bill laughed. "Literally, not figuratively. After the war he retired to Oakham, Massachusetts, purchased a farm, and lived a long life as a farmer. A couple of his kids moved to Rhode Island. One became my grandmother."

I paused to catch up.

"And you mentioned that you were an S.O.B."

"That I am. An inside joke. I have an ancestor who fought for Old Dixie. A great, great-grandfather on my mother's side served in the 36th North Carolina Coastal Artillery. Fought at Fort Fisher. I searched him on Ancestry. After the war he married a Connecticut woman who lived near the fort, so our family always got a kick thinking what he was really doing all day while on duty."

Bill Dunleavy reached for the peanuts with his thumb and three fingers.

"Darn things are addicting." He grabbed a second handful.

"And I got her ring." Alice held up her left hand and wiggled her fingers. "Bill gave me the same ring that his great, great-grandfather gave her, so I actually wear a Confederate bride's wedding band."

"So, you're from North Carolina then?"

"Tell him the story!" Alice jabbed at him with her elbow.

"Not at all. Another story. He stayed around Wilmington after the war. From what we've learned he and his wife worked with the local freed slave community during Reconstruction. They were sort of the nineteenth century version of community organizers, I guess.

"Anyway," Bill continued through a full mouth, "Wilmington was a pretty good bi-racial experiment right after the war. The city was mostly black. The city council was bi-racial, with about two thirds white and one-third black. There were both white and black thriving businesses.

"Then, in November 1898 the city elected a white Fusionist mayor. Two days after the election a white supremacist paramilitary unit called the Red Shirts overthrew the city council and seized power. I think it was the only time in our nation's history where there was a successful military *coup d'etat* of a constitutionally elected government."

"This happened when?"

"In 1898."

"Never heard of it."

"Where'd you grow up?" Alice demanded.

"Michigan."

She and her husband exchanged nods. "I would have thought they'd teach some black history up there. Same thing happened in New Orleans a few years earlier," she added. "In 1874, a paramilitary organization called the Crescent City White League, comprised mostly of Confederate Veterans, attempted to overthrow the Reconstruction government. The insurrection got put down after three days, but the City erected a monument to the so-called Battle of Liberty Place honoring the white supremacists that stood there until just recently."

"After the successful *coup d'etat* in Wilmington, the paramilitary installed its own all-white city council," Bill said. "They rampaged through the city. They burned down the Daily Record, the only black newspaper in North Carolina. They burned most of the black businesses. The white rioting lasted for days. Over one hundred leaders of the black community were dragged from their houses and murdered in the streets, and when the Red Shirts were done they'd driven twenty-one hundred black residents out of the city. Not one white was killed in the rioting. The freed blacks simply abandoned their homes and businesses, making what had been a successful bi-racial experiment into a virtual all-white enclave."

"It got worse," Alice added. "What happened in Wilmington became the model for white supremacy and segregation. The year after the Wilmington riots North Carolina passed a constitutional amendment making white supremacy state law. Segregation was mandated in all public facilities, and a slew of Jim Crow laws were enacted, from poll taxes as a prerequisite to voting to 'literacy tests' that could only be administered by white people."

"And your great-grandfather was involved?" I asked.

"Double great. In more ways than one. And yes, he was involved. He and other activists appealed to President McKinley to intercede, but the president wouldn't since the governor hadn't asked for assistance. McKinley ignored them all. States rights, you know."

"That was the beginning of official segregation in the South," Alice explained. "By the next year most of the old Confederate states had copied the Wilmington and North Carolina models, and Jim Crow became the law across the South."

"And your double great-grandfather?" I asked.

"He and my great, great-grandmother, who was some sort of spitfire herself, were driven out of Wilmington by the white supremacists. All the sympathetic whites got driven out. That's how that branch of my family ended up in Upstate New York."

"Wow," I said. "I never knew that story."

"Not many do. It's not talked about much," Bill added.

"Although I never met her," Alice said, "I admire the spunk of his wife, and am proud to wear her ring.

"But what about you?" she asked, changing gears. "You got a girl? A handsome fellow like yourself?"

"I do have a girlfriend, Anne. We've been dating for almost two years."

"What's she like?" Alice asked.

I smiled. "She's terrific. She's got a five-year old daughter who's as cute as can be. She shares custody with her ex, and they co-parent very well together."

"She live in Tampa?"

I nodded. "She's a middle school social studies teacher. Majored in history at Florida State and loves teaching that age group."

Alice sighed and shook her head. "Jason, you sound like a Census Survey. All demographics, ticked off box by box. Children, check. Marital status, check. Employment, check. Do you love her?"

The question took me aback. I wasn't offended so much as surprised. I had just met this woman who was older than my mother.

"You know, Jason,"—Bill shot a sideways look at his wife— "with these monuments it's not the facts of the war that are important. Those who want to keep the Confederate monuments don't need them to tell what happened at that spot. And those that want to build the Union monument at Olustee don't need it to record which units fought there. You can read facts in a book, or get them from a tour guide. These monuments are all about feelings, both for those who want them and those who oppose them. It's feelings that motivate people, not facts."

I took a deep breath. I'd likely never see these people again. Talking to them was almost like talking in the confessional.

"Yeah, I love her. I love her to death. She's different from every other girl I dated. It's not just that she's smart. She listens to me. She cares what I think, not just about my work but what I think every day. She gets it. And as much as anything else, I like who I am when I'm around her."

"So what's the problem I'm sensing?" Alice asked. "I haven't heard anything about a ring."

"Alice!"

Alice shushed her husband with a look and turned back to me.

I shrugged. "I don't know if I'm going to be able to stay around Florida much longer. I'm about to get a job offer—an incredible job offer from the Detroit Free Press as a political reporter. A real step up in my career. And with her shared custody Anne can't leave the state."

"You know," Bill said when I finished, "during the war, when men enlisted on either side, they didn't always do things because it was easy, or in their best economic or financial interest. Sometimes they acted because their heart told them to."

"So, this Civil War thing is pretty important to you?"

"There are a lot of interest groups on both sides," he said. "Union descendant groups, separate ones for men and women. Auxiliary groups. Groups for people who have an interest in the war even though no family member fought in it. Lots of re-enactor groups, although those seem to be falling off. The Confederate side has the same. Sons of Confederate Veterans, Daughters of the Confederacy. They're the ones put the first monuments up at the battlefield."

Bill Dunleavy helped himself to one of the finger sandwiches. When he next spoke, he did so deliberately.

"For me, it's a way to honor my ancestors' sacrifice, on both sides. And it is for many on the Confederate side, too. But recently, there's been an increase in interest on the Confederate side for reasons that have nothing to do with the war."

"Such as?" I perked up.

"You saw what happened at the school. The whole Confederate flag issue, the claim that they're victims of a large media-fueled push for 'political correctness,' targeting their Southern heritage. Wrapped up in that is an effort to redefine the Civil War as having had nothing to do with slavery. The phrase 'states' rights' gets tossed around more lately.

"Quite frankly," he said, speaking through another full mouth, "much of this came about after Obama's election. They'll deny it has anything to do with that, but America's changing—again—you know, ethnically and socially, and I think the whole Confederate flag crowd pines for a lifestyle that's disappearing. The Lost Cause nostalgia gives them a place where they share ideas with like-minded folks."

Still chewing, Bill Dunleavy stood and walked to a walnut bookcase against the far wall of his living room. He didn't hunt long before tugging down a book. When he returned he remained standing, thumbing through the hard-bound volume.

"Whenever there's something like there was at the school gymnasium, you always hear the argument that the Confederate flag, or in this case the opposition to a Union monument, has nothing to do with current social issues, but only with regional pride. You hear the argument that secession, and the establishment of the Confederate government, had nothing to do with slavery or white supremacy, and that the Confederate flag didn't stand for slavery and should not be considered offensive. Here it is."

He held the book in front of him and adjusted his eyeglasses. "This is from a speech given by Confederate Vice-President Alexander Stevens in Savannah, Georgia on March 21, 1861. This was after several states had seceded and adopted the new Confederate constitution, but before Sumter was fired on. It's known as the Cornerstone Speech and was given to explain the cornerstone reason why the slave states needed to form their own nation.

"In it Stevens said, and I quote," Bill continued, "'The new Constitution has put at rest forever all the agitating questions relating to our peculiar institutions—African slavery as it exists among us—the proper status of the negro in our form of civilization. This was the immediate cause of the late rupture and present revolution. Jefferson, in his forecast, had anticipated this, as the "rock upon which the old Union would split." He was right. What was conjecture with him, is now a realized fact. But whether he fully comprehended the great truth upon which that rock stood and stands, may be doubted. The prevailing ideas entertained by him and most of the leading statesmen at the time of the formation of the old Constitution were, that the enslavement of the African was in violation of the laws of nature; that it was wrong in principle, socially, morally and politically. It was an evil they knew not well how to deal with; but the general opinion of the men of that day was, that, somehow or other, in the order of Providence, the institution would be evanescent and pass away...

"'Those ideas, however, were fundamentally wrong. They rested upon the assumption of the equality of races. This was an error. It was a sandy foundation, and the idea of a Government built upon it—when the 'storm came, and the wind blew, it fell.

"'Our new Government is founded upon exactly the opposite ideas; its foundations are laid, its cornerstone rests, upon the great truth that the negro is not equal to the white man; that slavery, subordination to the superior race, is his natural and normal condition.'"

Softly closing the book, Bill Dunleavy returned it to its shelf.

"You can't get much clearer than that," he said, sitting again. "My ancestor in the 34th Massachusetts, and every other Union soldier, fought this war for one reason only, to prevent the establishment of a white supremacist nation in North America. Slavery and white supremacy were the only reason for secession and the adoption of the Confederate constitution, which prohibited the passage of any law that sought to abolish slavery."

"So much for states' rights," Alice smirked.

Bill nodded. "Many of the Confederate monuments at issue today were erected long after the war ended, in the late nineteenth century during the re-establishment of white control of the South, after World War I during a nascent civil rights movement, or in the nineteen fifties during de-segregation. That's why so many stand in front of courthouses, or town halls. They wanted to signal who was in charge. But now they want to say that the Confederacy, the Confederate flag, all that, had nothing to do with white supremacy."

Bill leaned forward. "It was no coincidence that Ronald Reagan gave his 1980 speech endorsing a revival of states rights in Neshoba County, Mississippi, the very county where those three young civil rights workers were murdered by the Klan and local cops just sixteen years earlier. At least my Confederate ancestor who fled Wilmington dealt with individuals whose actions and motives were transparent. I honor him for his service to his state during the war. But what he didn't know as he fought in defense of Fort Fisher in 1865, he certainly learned in 1898."

Bill took a deep breath. "Historians can come up with all sorts of political and economic rationalizations for historical events, but sometimes it just comes down to a simple question of what's in a person's soul, whether it's a presidential decision or a simple vote in a voting booth. The actions of people may be clear, but their real motives have become easier to mask, wouldn't you say?"

"And Agnes Thornberry?" I asked, avoiding a direct response. "Would you put her in that category?"

Both Dunleavys shook their heads.

"Hardly," Alice answered, covering her mouth to prevent food spillage.

Bill put down his sandwich. "I tell you what, why don't we take a ride over to her place tomorrow before you go back? It's supposed to rain anyway. Maybe together we can complete that story you're looking for. She knows the personal side of what happened at Olustee as well as any historian. It's an oral history passed down through her family. I know a bit about the military side of things. When you look at what happened on the day of the battle, you have to begin with the Union troops muster at Barber Plantation that morning. The night before had been cold..."

CHAPTER 13

8th Regiment, United States Colored Troops
Barber Plantation
28 miles west of Jacksonville
12 miles east of Sanderson
Saturday, February 20, 1864
Dawn

Private Charles Dunhill had not slept well. The night air was freezing, and the cold crept up from the ground through his bedroll and stiffened his bones. He was reluctant to turn over, lest his tent mates realize he was not asleep and sensed the icy hand that gripped his stomach. He knew they were afraid too. But talking about it was seen as a sure sign of cowardice. Better to keep it inside and exhibit a devil-may-care attitude.

When his unit's bugle sounded he jumped up and stumbled outside. From around the plantation other bugles summoned their troops. Men emerged from tents, tugging on shirts and jerseys, fumbling over their weapons and gear. A line of soldiers snaked to the latrines behind the pines at the edge of the cleared space. This was an army preparing to move.

Colonel Charles Fribley, commander of the 8th United States Colored Troops, was fully dressed in great coat and belted sword. Charles Dunhill wondered if he had slept any better. He studied his commanding officer's face, searching for an indication of his confidence level.

Charles Fribley had risen through the ranks from non-commissioned officer to captain by the fall of 1863. When the opportunity presented itself to make colonel by accepting command of a colored regiment, Fribley had seized it, and had commanded the 8th since the prior November. There were 575 officers and men of the 8th Colored Regiment, and they would be going into battle in the next two days for the first time under the leadership of a man with no regimental command experience.

But Fribley's face betrayed nothing. Maybe white people just have more confidence, Charles reasoned.

The unit's second-in-command, Major Burritt, strode among the troops, loudly instructing them to load up, and get their backpacks on. "It'll be a long march, and we need be ready to fight."

Sergeants tied red sashes around their waists. The sashes would serve as visible signs of authority midst the expected chaos.

Lieutenant Oliver Norton approached the area in front of the tent where Charles Dunhill hunched over, checking his pack.

"Charles," Norton said in a low voice.

Charles turned. Lieutenant Norton was the only white officer who ever called him by his first name. The lieutenant took him by the arm and led him away from the tent.

"We'll be marching west today," he said. The lieutenant looked around to assure no one else could hear. Soldiers were rolling up their bedding and strapping it to the top of their backpacks. Others struck the tents and rolled them along the ground into white cylindrical shapes. Each man would carry a rifle, ammunition, a day's rations, water, and bedroll, but the tents were loaded onto wagons that would trail the army.

The lieutenant moved Charles further from the hubbub spreading across the plantation.

"The men like you," the lieutenant said, "and respect you. I'll say this straight up. I wanted you as one of my sergeants, or at least a corporal in my company, but Major Burritt and the colonel have final say. No matter what happens today, I need to rely on you to keep the men together. Keep them calm, and make sure they handle their weapons right. And for God's sake man, use your common sense no matter what happens or who says what. Do I make myself plain?"

"Yes, sir," Charles answered, although he was not sure. "But Corporal Cotton, sir—"

"—is a good man," Norton finished. "I'm looking to you for help today." The lieutenant clapped the private on the shoulder and turned back to where the regiment's cook heated coffee over an open fire.

Private Charles Dunhill turned in the opposite direction and went off to the latrines. When he returned the tents were down. The white cylinders had been trundled across the field to the supply wagons already hitched to their teams.

When a cook lifted a pot of coffee at him he waved it off. Coffee made him pee, and he didn't want that distraction during a long march.

He grabbed hardtack and cornmeal and munched without washing them down. On impulse, he took a slice of desiccated vegetables, the term given to dehydrated, shredded vegetables packed in cakes.

The sun was up, and Charles Dunhill couldn't see one cloud in the sky. Despite the freezing night, perhaps today was going to be warm, yet not too hot to march comfortably. A perfect Florida winter day. At least for the weather, he thought grimly.

Lieutenant Norton and the sergeants yelled for everyone to form up by companies. Charles hustled into line.

"Ain't it grand?" Private Jeffers shouldered up next to him. "You think we be fighting rebs today?"

"Today or tomorrow. We probably won't make Lake City before night."

"I thought we fighting today," a soldier behind called out.

"Lake City is 33 miles," Charles answered without twisting around. "We can march fifteen, maybe twenty miles in a day, but we can't make Lake City."

"Sure we can," another soldier answered. "Why, back in Pennsylvania, when we in camp, we done march thirty miles one day."

"That was camp," Charles retorted. "Now's we got gear and rifles. We could do thirty and make Lake City, if we want to show up after sunset, in the dark, too tired to stand. And then tomorrow we be too tired to fight."

"Attention, men!" Colonel Fribley called out. He strode up and down the regiment, now assembled in lines by company, looking over each soldier. "As most of you know, we're heading for the bridge over the Suwanee River. That river is just beyond Lake City, and Lake City is where the Florida militia is camped. To get to the river we need to get through Lake City. To capture that bridge we have to defeat the rebs holding it. When we do, that is the last rebel camp in north Florida. We capture that, capture that bridge, that'll cut Florida off from Georgia. The whole rebel army in Virginia gets their beef from Florida. We capture that bridge and their rebel army up north is going to run out of food pretty quick.

"Gentlemen," he continued. "This march, and battle, could end this war."

Several soldiers let out boisterous huzzahs.

"I don't expect we'll reach Lake City today," the colonel continued. "More likely tomorrow. But there may be militia cavalry about, so we might have skirmishing. I need everybody to keep a sharp eye."

Across the plantation other regimental commanders were addressing their troops, raised voices piercing the morning air.

Lieutenant Norton directed the regiment's fife and drummers forward. Boys as young as fourteen raced to the head of the regiment behind the color bearers. A light breeze caught both the Stars and Stripes and the regimental flag. A good omen? Charles wondered.

The men of the 8th remained in formation as the army got underway. The road to the west passed in front of where they stood, and Charles Dunhill watched as Colonel Henry's cavalry trotted out in the lead, the men riding two abreast. General Seymour, sitting high on horseback, led the infantry out next, accompanied by his aides and flag bearers. First in line behind the general was Hawley's Brigade, consisting of the New Hampshire and Connecticut 7th infantries. After they passed, the 8th turned and joined the brigade at its rear. Behind the 8th marched Barton's Brigade of New Yorkers and Montgomery's Brigade of two colored regiments: the 1st North Carolina Colored Volunteers and the Massachusetts 54th.

"That's the 54th Massachusetts behind us," Jim Jeffers said to no one in particular. "I guess they must like us better, putting us more in the front."

"Not all the 54th," Corporal Cotton answered from the edge of the formation. "General Seymour left behind two companies of the 54th to guard the railway and man the blockhouses."

"And I hear a detachment from the First North Carolina Colored also got left behind," Jeffers added.

"They all be escaped slaves from North Carolina, some from Virginia, just formed up." Corporal Cotton looked out into the woods.

"How soon they just formed up?" a soldier in front asked.

"Not long," the corporal answered.

"So, they never been in battle neither," Charles said.

"How many of us we got altogether?" the soldier in the rear asked. "I mean white and black."

"A New Hampshire boy was saying we got over four thousand, plus fourteen pieces of artillery," Jeffers answered.

"Should be plenty to whip them rebs," the first soldier predicted.

Just west of Barber's Plantation the wagon track narrowed. The soldiers of the 8th adjusted their formation, reducing to six abreast. Pine branches tore at the soldiers on the flanks, and soon the column reduced to just four abreast.

The air continued to warm in the morning sun, and the fife and drums at the head of the regiment struck up a series of patriotic songs, beginning with "The John Brown Song," followed by the "Battle Hymn of The Republic" and "Battle Cry of Freedom." By demand of the troops, the fife and drummers kept returning to "The John Brown Song." The men who knew the words joined in the singing, teaching those who did not. Charles Dunhill felt his spirits begin to lift.

CHAPTER 14

7th New Hampshire Volunteer Regiment
On the road from Barber Plantation to Lake City
Saturday, February 20, 1864
Mid-morning

Sergeant Richard Colburn hadn't slept much that night. In addition to his usual pre-battle angst, he had concerns over the new men and the unit's weapons.

But as the 7th New Hampshire trudged along the winding road out of Barber Plantation, the sergeant was satisfied that the unit was peppered with a corps of veterans. It was raised in Manchester in the summer of 1861 by Joseph Abbott, a local lawyer and newspaper editor. In October, Governor Berry had appointed Colonel Haldimand Sumner Putnam, an experienced army officer, to command the regiment. Lt. Colonel Joseph Abbot was placed second in command.

The regiment recruited throughout the late fall and drilled in Manchester. Colonel Putnam, a strict disciplinarian, emphasized drill and weapons handling. He was a firm proponent that under the duress of battle the more disciplined side would prevail. Despite his insistence on strict regimen, the men of the 7th, all volunteers, liked him.

In January the regiment left Manchester for New York City for four weeks of drilling. The next month, the unit left New York for duty on the Dry Tortugas—seven lonely, desolate islands west of the Florida Keys serving as a storage and distribution center for the Union forts in the South.

The trip from New York had proved more hazardous than duty in the Keys. In the New York camp, soldiers assembled from around the east coast brought their own diseases. Latrines overflowed and reeked. Soldiers took sick with coughs and viruses. When it came time to embark on the *USS Tycoon* dozens of soldiers, unfit to travel, were left behind.

Conditions aboard ship were worse, and in the cramped spaces below decks almost every man took ill. When they finally landed in Key West, the soldiers learned that the half of the regiment aboard the *USS Mallory* had not fared better.

The regiment moved to Fort Jefferson where they spent the next three and a half months loading and unloading supply ships as military cargo arrived from the northeast to be redistributed to the Union's southern forts. When not working as stevedores, the 7th marched, drilled, rebuilt and strengthened the fortifications of Fort Jefferson, and stood endless guard duty. Time off was spent hunting bird and turtle eggs and exploring nearby islands.

Just when the unit had recovered its physical health the regiment was ordered to Beaufort, South Carolina. They returned to Key West to await transport. While waiting among the teeming swarm of soldiers in the busy transport hub, the first signs of yet another virus appeared. Soldiers from other units began complaining of fever, nausea, and chills. After four or five days some of the soldiers appeared to improve, only a day later to have their skin turn yellow. The men of the 7th not showing symptoms were loaded aboard ships bound for Beaufort. Aboard the *USS Ben Deford,* several soldiers from the 7th were diagnosed with Yellow Fever. After landing in South Carolina the health of the regiment worsened, and it again lost its effectiveness as a fighting force.

"Sergeant, I have to pee."

It was one of the new recruits seeking guidance on how to handle a call to nature while on a quick march.

Sergeant Colburn examined the road ahead. The 7th marched in a line at the front of Hawley's Brigade, at the head of an army of five thousand five hundred men. Only Henry's Cavalry was in front of them to watch for the enemy. Whenever the road straightened out, giving him a clear view to the west, the sergeant could see the cavalry a half mile ahead.

The road narrowed even more, forcing the soldiers to march just three abreast. At the head of the infantry General Seymour rode with his staff, followed by Colonel Abbott.

"Run up along the side of this track," the sergeant directed, "and get ahead of the men. But don't get ahead of the general. Take your rifle and pack with you. When you're done join your line as we pass by."

The private ran up along the right side of the column, holding his rifle with his left hand and covering his head with his right to keep his kepi in place.

Although the men grumbled about marching, Sergeant Colburn never minded it. It was better than garrison busywork, and far better than parade drilling. On a distance march he reasoned that at least the unit was going somewhere.

Marching men had a sense of camaraderie absent in campfire discussions or after-hours tent talk. In a march, everyone shared equally in the physical exertion, while struggling to reach the common goal. He had come to appreciate the regular sound of the march, the steady line of blue-clad soldiers clanking in rhythm as slung bayonets banged against ammo pouches, canteens, and personal mess tins.

Just before noon, the blue line snaked past dilapidated houses and shanties.

Private Frink sidled up alongside.

"This ain't the South I saw in my dreams when I signed up," he said, with an almost wide-eyed expression.

"What is it you imagined, Private?" Sergeant Colburn watched a mangy dog peer out from a half-collapsed porch.

"I thought the South was all big, huge mansions, with tall white columns and hundreds of darkies running about carrying food and drink to the white owners."

"Well, Private, I suppose there're plenty of houses like that, what you imagined when you thought of the South. Probably mostly in Virginia or Georgia, but this is Florida, son, not the South of the stories you heard growing up. These people are poor."

"I just don't understand it, Sergeant, why people in this part of the country even support the rebels. They got nothing down here, 'cepting mosquitoes." He swatted at his face.

"You know, Sergeant, if any of these shacks were back in Chester, we'd burn them for kindling and build a decent house. Even the poorest of folks in my town wouldn't live like this. And the land, all pine, not a decent place to plant a crop."

The private slapped again at the buzzing around his face.

"And that's another thing, Sergeant. It's these damn bugs, if you pardon my language. I ain't never seen bugs like this afore. Even in the early summer, when they're at their worst. I can't but wonder why these people don't pull up stakes and move north."

A soldier marching behind laughed aloud. "Well, Private, why don't you ask them yourself. Here's one."

Twenty yards ahead, an elderly man stood at the left edge of the dusty trail. Clad in a torn shirt, and disheveled trousers, he leaned on a cane as he studied the Union soldiers move past.

"Y'all be careful," he said to no one in particular. "There's rebels up ahead, lots of them."

Lieutenant Preston stepped out of line and confronted the civilian.

"Oh yeah? How you saying?"

"I seen them yesterday," the old man retorted. "West of here. Cavalry. Weren't no scouts, neither. Maybe a whole company. I ain't no traitor; I'm loyal to the Union. Cavalry that big, why, there had to be infantry behind them, close by."

Sergeant Colburn stepped out of line and joined the pair.

"How you know that, grandpa?" the sergeant asked. As soldiers walked past he moved closer to the civilian to make room. There was liquor on the old man's breath.

"I seen them yesterday, just up this here road." The old man pulled a kerchief from his pocket and wiped the dust from his eyes. "I tell you, it was at least a whole company. They don't send no cavalry down this far 'less they got a reason."

"Florida militia?" the lieutenant asked. The old man shook his head.

"I know militia cavalry when I see them. I've seen the Florida 2nd Cavalry before. This weren't no militia. This was Georgia Cavalry. Confederate regulars."

On the opposite side of the road the private who had run ahead to relieve himself emerged from the woods, tugging at his trousers. He raced to catch up with his comrades. The other men laughed.

"Mosquito bite you?" one asked, to more laughter.

Sergeant Colburn rejoined his soldiers.

"You believe that old drunk?" a deep voiced soldier in the front asked.

"I don't know," the sergeant called back. "He says he knows cavalry, says there was a lot. Not just scouts."

"Any word there's Georgia cavalry about?" another soldier asked. "We been told there was only militia."

Other soldiers weighed in. "No one else seen any regular Confederate Army around these parts," a corporal concluded.

Lieutenant Preston ran past the soldiers on their left, racing up the line toward Colonel Abbott.

"We gonna' rest soon?" Private Frink asked. "We been marching for hours."

"There's no good place to rest," the sergeant answered. "'Less we spread out in the yards of some of these shacks. But sitting on the ground this crowded with pine trees up close is not the safest place if that old man's reports of rebel army be true."

The ironic thing, the sergeant thought even as he spoke, was that resting had never been safe for the 7th. While resting in South Carolina in the summer of 1862 the health of the regiment deteriorated further as the ravages of Yellow Fever tore through the unit.

By August the 7th was so weakened that it was ordered to St. Augustine. The city was hailed as the healthiest spot in the South. By that time the regiment had lost over 200 men to disease since leaving Manchester seven months earlier, and none to enemy fire.

In St. Augustine, the 7th relieved four garrisoned companies of Colonel Bell's 4th New Hampshire. The 7th was no longer considered fit for duty.

There the unit began to recover. New recruits arrived from New Hampshire to restore the unit to full strength. Soldiers rested while still practicing shooting and combat maneuvers, and performing guard and picket duty. There was little rebel activity in the St. Augustine area, and the unit patrolled the city without challenge.

They spent a pleasant winter in the city, and by April 1863, when the regiment was ordered to Fernandina, just outside Jacksonville, the 7th was again at full strength and fully equipped, a well-disciplined unit looking for its first fight.

They stayed in Fernandina for two months. In June, the regiment boarded the steamer *USS Boston* bound for Hilton Head, South Carolina.

They made camp on Folly Island. A few miles away Fort Wagner, at the northern tip of Morris Island, guarded the southern approach to Charleston Harbor. Its capture was crucial to the Union plan to take Charleston and close the port.

A battery at the island's southern tip protected the fort from a land attack from the rear. Landing just a few hundred yards away, the 7th New Hampshire quickly overran the rebel batteries. They spread out and fought their way across the island, taking just three hours to capture two-thirds of it. Only their objective of Fort Wagner remained, now reinforced by boats from Charleston.

On July 17, the 7th New Hampshire attacked the fort, but were repelled. The next day, the 7th supported the 54th Massachusetts Regiment's attack on the bastion.

The results were devastating. Although both the 54th and the 7th gained a temporary foothold within the fort, they were beaten back with great loss of life in both units. The 54th's Colonel Robert Gould Shaw was killed in the assault, as was the 7th's Colonel Putnam. The 7th lost 216 men and officers that day.

Although unsuccessful, members of the 7th, in tandem with the 54th's, became legendary throughout the North. For the duration of the summer of 1863, other soldiers would remove their hats and shout huzzahs whenever either the 7th or 54th passed by.

Colonel Joseph Abbott was named the new commander of the regiment, and it soon became known as Abbott's Regiment, and its soldiers as "Abbott's Boys."

Five miles west of Barber's Plantation Sergeant Colburn heard the unmistakable clanking of a regiment rapidly approaching from the rear. The soldiers of the 7th gathered in close in the middle of the road as the 7th Connecticut, led by Captain Benjamin F. Skinner, double-timed past on both sides and assumed the lead position in the march.

"Colonel Seymour wants the 7th Connecticut in front." Lieutenant Preston brushed dust from his trousers. "They have Spencer repeating carbines and may encounter the enemy first."

"And we do not," the sergeant added.

After the Connecticut men passed, the 7th New Hampshire resumed its march. Ahead, the Connecticut regiment continued double-timing in an effort to catch up to the Union cavalry. Rounding a bend in the dusty road, Sergeant Colburn saw that both the Union cavalry and the Connecticut regiment were no longer in view.

"That didn't look like no regiment to me," a veteran New Hampshire soldier grumbled.

"It's not," another one answered. "They're down to four companies. Less than four hundred men."

"And a captain in charge," added a third soldier.

"Yeah, but they got them nice rifles," the second shot back. "Gives them the power of a brigade."

"We used to have them," the first soldier groused. "But they took them from us."

"And give us garbage in return," the second said, to general laughter.

At noon the regiment stopped at a farm in Sanderson, spreading out in the field, removing their shoes, and breaking out their food rations.

"You Union boys be stepping pretty good going west," a young woman called out when they stood to resume their march. "But in a few hours you'll be coming back faster than you're goin', running for your lives."

CHAPTER 15

7th Connecticut Infantry Regiment
On the road from Barber Plantation to Lake City
West of Sanderson
Saturday, February 20, 1864
Early afternoon

Captain Benjamin F. Skinner was not as confident about his regiment as were the other soldiers at Barber Plantation who had gawked at the Connecticut men with envy. The captain understood the stares. The Spencer rifles could fire seven cartridges to the musket's one.

The previous fall the regiment's then-commander, Colonel Joseph Hawley, had lobbied for the unit to get Spencers to replace their Springfields. Ultimately, he had convinced Major General Alfred Terry.

Hawley had advantages in his lobbying. Alfred Terry, the former New Haven lawyer and court clerk, had raised the regiment of a thousand men and officers in September 1861 in New Haven, and been appointed its first commander. Although not a West Point graduate, Terry had proved such an able commander that he had quickly risen to the rank of Major General. Upon Terry's ascension, Lieutenant Colonel Joseph Hawley had assumed command of the 7th Connecticut. He had so impressed his superiors that he was soon given his own brigade to command, comprised of the 7th Connecticut, the 7th New Hampshire, and the 8th United States Colored Regiment.

After training, the 7th Connecticut had spent the entire war assigned to the Department of the South. It had fought in the siege of Fort Pulaski, and the battles of Secessionville and Battery Wagner. Like the 7th New Hampshire, in 1863 the Connecticut 7th was part of the garrison of St. Augustine and guarded the rail head at Fernandina.

The Connecticut 7th had served in so many of the same places simultaneously as the New Hampshire 7th, that the pair were affectionately referred to as The New England 77th. The regiments also trained together the previous summer at Folly Island in South Carolina.

In October of 1863, the Connecticut 7th was reclassified as "boat infantry," and trained to make an amphibious assault on Fort Sumter. While prepping for this assault Hawley succeeded in getting Spencers for the regiment. Although the Sumter plan was eventually deemed impractical and abandoned, the Connecticut unit kept their new rifles.

But Skinner knew that repeating rifles could only compensate for so much. In January, to encourage re-enlistments, the 7th Connecticut had allowed over three hundred of its soldiers, and eleven veteran officers, thirty-day furloughs to return home. Although the unit received an infusion of 112 replacements in return, the new soldiers were ill-trained, unproven, and comprised mostly of substitutes, draftees and foreigners who spoke no English. Morale quickly deteriorated. Rumors of fights and knife assaults between enlisted personnel ran rampant through the ranks.

By the time the Connecticut 7th set off from Barber Plantation that morning, it was under four hundred men strong, and promotions of its former commanders had left Benjamin Skinner in charge. The captain reorganized the regiment into a battalion-size force of four slightly undersized companies. As a captain, he was the lowest ranked officer leading a regiment west that day.

Despite these problems, within five miles of departure General Seymour had sent the Connecticut regiment to the lead in support of Henry's Cavalry. Captain Skinner had marched his men on the double-quick, past the New Hampshire 7th, getting his regiment a half mile in front of the army's main body.

They rested briefly in Sanderson, and then, to stay in front, had left before the balance of the army arrived. Where the dirt road crossed the railroad line west of Sanderson, Captain Skinner followed orders and advanced his four companies up the rail line.

The railroad bed was wider than the dirt road. The captain was thankful, for he preferred not advancing in as narrow a column as the road dictated. A narrow column afforded little protection should they encounter the enemy.

Captain Skinner heard the galloping before he spotted the approaching cavalry soldier.

"Sir," the rider said, saluting while reining in his mount. "Orders from General Seymour. You are to send two of your companies ahead, one on each side of this rail bed. Fan them out in a skirmish line. Your other two companies are to advance behind them in column formation."

Skinner was confused.

"We're only three miles out of Sanderson, not even half way to Lake City. Walking through the pines will tire the men."

"The general has received reports of Confederate cavalry in the area."

The captain acknowledged. As the rider rode off, Captain Skinner ordered two companies to the fore and told them to spread out.

Less than a mile later Captain Skinner heard scattered musket shots. He raised his right arm to signal a halt, and the two companies marching behind him clanked to a stop.

Lieutenant Robert Dempsey approached.

The captain was tempted to order the two companies into battle line, but there was insufficient room in the narrow rail bed.

"Not our skirmishers, sir," the lieutenant said.

"No?"

The lieutenant pointed up the rail line. Two hundred yards ahead soldiers from his deployed companies still crept along the rail bed. The soldiers swiveled their heads side to side, rifles held out in front with both hands.

"That must be the 1st Massachusetts Cavalry," Skinner said. "They must have encountered Confederate cavalry."

"Or perhaps the 40th Massachusetts Mounted Infantry," Dempsey suggested. "They're both on the flanks."

"Whoever it is, it's not a main body." Skinner raised his hand signaling the column forward. Seeing the companies behind them resume their march, the Connecticut skirmishers called to their comrades, and the two Union lines in the woods continued their own advance.

CHAPTER 16

4th Georgia Cavalry
East of Olustee

Captain Frederick Mallory also heard the rifle fire. Like his Union counterpart, he called a halt to his command.

General Joseph Finnigan's orders had been clear. The 4th Georgia Cavalry was to find and engage the forward Union units and fight a light, retreating skirmish, drawing the Yankees back to the Confederate earthworks. If the federals could be led to Camp Beauregard, the Confederates could wage a defensive battle from behind their newly constructed fort. The camp was far enough east of Olustee that swamps to the north and south would keep the federals from swinging around to attack their flank.

Captain Mallory assumed that Lieutenant Colonel Abner McCormick's 2nd Florida Cavalry had located the Union skirmishers.

"Orders, sir?" a sergeant asked, nudging his mount alongside.

"Can't see a damn thing in these woods," Mallory replied. "That firing's coming from our right. Let's move that way."

"Sir!" the sergeant barked, pointing. "There's movement in the woods."

Mallory wrenched his field glasses from his belt.

"Union Cavalry," he announced. "We'll pull back and report their position to General Colquitt."

A private ducked under a branch and rode up to the captain.

"Sir, word from General Finnigan. The general sent Harrison's 64th Georgia Infantry Regiment and two companies of the 32nd Georgia infantry forward. They're going to form a battle line just back from the first cross-road where the road and train line cross. We're to engage the enemy and then slowly fall back on this line and form on both sides of the infantry."

Mallory nodded. "That'll draw the Yankees back to the breastworks. Get them to attack our fortifications."

The private shook his head. "Yes, sir, I know that was the plan, but the general ordered the forward line reinforced. It seems like he's going to make a stand in the woods instead of at Camp Beauregard."

"Are you sure, Private?" Mallory demanded, twisting around.

"As sure as I'm sitting on this saddle, sir. General Finnegan ordered up General Colquitt's 6th, 19th and 28th Georgia Infantry Regiments. Artillery too. He's forming a battle line in the woods, miles in front of the earthworks we built last night."

Mallory swore. "That's four regiments out of eight. Damn!"

Mallory heard a heavy volley followed by cracking branches as Minié balls slammed into the trees above him.

"Fall back!" he commanded. "Fire as we move."

Already his cavalry company had begun their turn, moving west between the pines, turning and firing as they retreated.

General Seymour's Union Command
Four miles west of Sanderson

General Seymour was slouched over his horse's neck studying a map when the sounds of musketry intensified.

"Bring up Elder's Battery," he commanded an aide. When the artillery was wheeled into place the general ordered a barrage laid down in the trees beyond the forward skirmishing. He suspected it was more than retreating rebel pickets exchanging fire with federal cavalry. The reports from messengers was of rebel cavalry in the woods. But the last report claimed that a deployed Confederate battle line stretched across the woods less than a mile in front of him.

The officers surrounding the general covered their ears with their hands as the Union's Napoleons fired. Their horses neighed and backed at the sound of the cannons. Only practiced hands kept them from bolting.

The Union projectiles whooshed through the air and arced into the trees. Seymour heard the familiar sound of cracking tree limbs followed by the detonation of exploding shells. But instead of the expected lessening of musket fire, he heard explosions from Confederate cannons. Artillery shells flew into the woods around him, one falling directly in front of his aides. The horse next to the general reared back, toppling a young lieutenant, before galloping down the road, empty saddle, stirrups flapping.

Seymour swallowed. This was not cavalry pickets, or unsupported infantry.

"Corporal!" he called to a messenger. "Get to the rail line. Tell Captain Skinner to form all four of his companies in a battle line stretched to the right of the rail line. He's to capture those Confederate batteries!"

The general spun and grabbed two other messengers.

"Get ahead to the New Hampshire 7th," he told a second one. "Find Colonel Abbott. Tell him to advance in support of the Connecticut 7th.

"And you." He turned to the third messenger. "Find Colonel Fribley. Have him bring his coloreds into a battle line on the Connecticut's left, just to the left of our own artillery. Form strong battle lines all the way across. The coloreds need to protect the Connecticut's left as well as our artillery.

"Now go, all three of you!" he commanded as the messengers scampered off.

The general leaned back in his saddle. "I have no idea what the rebels have ahead," he muttered to his aides. "It sounds like they may not have stayed in Lake City after all. We'll need to get ready for anything."

CHAPTER 17

Captain Benjamin F. Skinner did not believe the order.

"Are you sure, Corporal?" he demanded of the young messenger.

The soldier, a lad no more than eighteen, nodded his head vigorously.

"That's what the general said, sir. The Lord's own truth. You're to advance on the rebel battery and capture it. It's pounding the column on the road, and the general says it needs to be captured."

The pair stood aside the rail bed. Behind the captain, two companies of the 7th Infantry Regiment stood patiently. Ahead, his other two companies had halted their advance. In twos and threes, soldiers ambled out of the woods, restlessly glancing back at the stalled advance. Confederate artillery whooshed overhead.

It wasn't the lad's fault, and there was no sense making him feel more uncomfortable than he already was. The captain adopted a conciliatory tone.

"Did the general happen to mention where this rebel artillery happens to be?" He hoped his voice did not sound sarcastic.

The lad shook his head. "No, sir," he stammered. "But it must be up ahead, mustn't it?"

Captain Skinner studied the rail line. More of his soldiers emerged from the woods. A large group milled about, facing back in confusion. If rebels were to advance through the tree lines now, they'd walk right up behind his whole regiment.

"Yes, up ahead, Corporal, but where in these damn woods? One can't ascertain the position of enemy artillery, Corporal, from the sound of shells passing overhead."

He didn't mention that enemy artillery would be guarded by infantry.

"Did the general say how large a battery he anticipates the rebels to have?" Perhaps he could pry an additional tidbit. The size of the battery might dictate how much infantry supported it.

The lad again shook his head.

"What about our own support, Corporal? Did he say whether we would have any for our attack?"

The corporal's eyes lit up. "No, sir. But I heard his orders to two other messengers. The 7th New Hampshire is to be directly behind you, and Colonel Fribley's 8th Colored on your left. Just to the left of our own artillery."

Captain Skinner nodded. The corporal should have told him this immediately. Still, if the lad hadn't been specifically instructed to tell him…

"Thank you, Corporal. Tell the general we'll form up and advance as ordered."

Without waiting to see the corporal race back toward General Seymour's command, Captain Skinner called to his nearest sergeant, and instructed him to round up the regiment's lieutenants. He turned back to his two-company column and ordered it to advance and link up with the forward companies.

When his lieutenants assembled he explained the situation cryptically.

"I want all four of our companies in the woods to our right. Shoulder to shoulder in a battle line. There's no need to divide the men into separate groups for firing and reloading. We have repeating rifles. A single line will suffice."

The officers nodded glumly.

"We advance as one line, all four companies. I will be in the middle. Advance on my command. Is that clear?"

When they nodded again Skinner added, "And lieutenants, control the firing rate of the men. I don't want everyone emptying their carbines at once in these damn pines. We need to keep a reserve of ammunition."

The officers ran off to meet with their sergeants. Captain Skinner hurried up the rail line to his forward companies. The men lounged about, their rifles resting on the ground.

"We're going forward. We'll advance in these woods to our right and capture the rebel artillery battery."

"How big?" a veteran asked. "Do we know their size?"

"It doesn't matter." Skinner turned away as he spoke. "We've got the best weaponry in the world."

The soldiers picked their way through the woods, officers positioning them three feet apart. Older veterans shoved new recruits into place. When the line formed up a lieutenant ran up to Captain Skinner and saluted.

"Men are in position, sir."

The captain nodded. He moved to the middle of the line and drew his sword. He held it aloft and looked down both lines. The pines prevented a clear view, but he estimated that his lines extended two hundred yards in each direction. The men stood ready, rifles held in front.

Captain Skinner pointed his sword to the west.

"Forward, advance!" he commanded, and the blue line stepped off.

Lieutenants and sergeants shouted corrections to keep the line straight as it surged forward. The captain saw only a solid stand of pine before him. He was grateful the underbrush was thin. Brambles and bushes would catch at the soldier's trousers, slowing their advance.

When the line had moved thirty yards a Union soldier shouted, "There!"

To the captain's right five rebel horsemen maneuvered behind the pines ahead. Shots rang out, and bark dropped from tree branches above. The horsemen retreated.

"Steady!" the captain commanded, and the line inched forward.

A second group of enemy cavalry appeared to their left. This time there were at least twenty, and they returned fire when the left of the Union line discharged a practiced volley. Anguished cries from both sides confirmed shots had struck, but the rebels again retreated.

When Union soldiers on the left broke into a trot, threatening to break the line, their lieutenants screamed at them to slow up.

"The rebel artillery must be straight ahead," a sergeant next to Captain Skinner announced with confidence. "Guarded by cavalry, not infantry."

"Did you get a look at the uniforms?" the captain asked.

"Why, rebel uniforms, sir."

The captain shook his head. "I know they were rebel, Sergeant. I thought I saw two types. Florida militia to our left, and maybe regular Confederate Cavalry to our right."

"There's no Confederate regulars around here, Captain."

"Tell that to the fellows in those uniforms."

"Here they come again!" another officer screamed. Over forty mounted riders emerged from the pines and fired as one at the advancing blue line. The return fire from the repeating rifles was withering, and several rebel riders toppled to the ground, their cries echoing between the trees.

"After them!" an officer shouted as the gray horsemen retreated.

The main body of cavalry had to be just ahead, with the artillery just behind. Captain Skinner lifted his sword to his shoulder and moved at the double quick, intent on not losing sight of the enemy. They would lead him to the big guns.

Other pockets of Confederate riders appeared, only to quickly withdraw under the barrage from the Union Spencers.

The horsemen ducking among the trees divided, with half breaking to the right and the rest to the left. Captain Skinner screamed a halt. Directly before him, through the trees, he saw a Confederate regimental flag next to a Confederate battle flag. Swiveling hard to his right he spotted another regimental flag.

A lieutenant touched his arm. "Sir, on the left, I count at least three regiments of infantry. And by the length of their line, it looks like full-size units."

"Another two to the right," a sergeant confirmed, pointing.

"Hold your position!" Skinner screamed in both directions, and the order echoed down the line.

The blue advance staggered to a halt, and some Union soldiers knelt in the wire grass. Others moved behind the nearest pine.

"At least five regiments," the lieutenant said. "In battle line."

"And guarded on both sides by that cavalry," the sergeant added.

"It's two cavalries," Skinner announced. "They split. The militia went one way, but they've got regular cavalry to our right."

"I see them," the lieutenant said, peering through his own field glasses. "That's not Florida militia. I can see their regimental flags."

The lieutenant adjusted his focus. "That's the 6th Georgia right in front of us. Maybe the 32nd Georgia to their right..."

He swung his binoculars left. "And over there it looks like the 64th Georgia, then the 28th further down."

"And that's the 4th Georgia Cavalry to our right," the sergeant added, pointing again. "They're the ones led us through these woods. They went one way and Florida Cavalry formed up on the other side of their infantry."

"Damn!" Skinner too dropped to a knee on the pine needles and squinted. Officers and sergeants crouched down with him.

"That's Colquitt out there," the captain said. "You're right. This is no Florida militia. We better get word back—"

Gunfire from the right exploded, quickly intensifying into a rapid exchange.

"What's happening?" the captain demanded, standing again, but moving deftly behind a pine.

Word soon passed down the line.

"Georgia Cavalry, sir!" a runner huffed. "They tried to flank us but we drove them off. They weren't expecting repeating rifles, and even at the flank we got a powerful lot of fire on them."

"Any sign of Abbott?" the captain demanded.

His officers shook their heads in unison.

"They've got to be right behind us. Can't see anything through these damn pines. Our orders are to take that battery, gentlemen. We have no choice."

"It's at least five regiments, Captain," Lieutenant Seward said. "Supported on both sides by cavalry."

"It is," Skinner agreed, "but our four companies have the fire power of a brigade. Have the men load up. We'll advance in a straight line. Keep up a constant barrage, and force them back. Keep the edges alert to any effort to flank us with cavalry."

The lieutenants and sergeants scattered. Soldiers loaded and checked their weapons.

"The New Hampshire 7th will hear our advance," Skinner said. "Abbott'll be here soon."

CHAPTER 18

4th Georgia Cavalry

Captain Frederick Mallory was stunned that the attempt to flank the Yankee right had failed. Everything else had gone so well.

The 4th Georgia Cavalry, and the 2nd Florida Cavalry, had implemented the plan to perfection. They had spotted the Yankees advancing in a line stretched through the woods, with no support, and had demonstrated against the federals in a series of feints that baited the Yankees to chase. The Confederate cavalries had pulled back, the Yankees in pursuit, until the federals were drawn opposite five entrenched regiments of Colquitt's Brigade.

The two Confederate cavalries had split, with the Georgia 4th moving back to its right, turning, and setting up a defensive perimeter at the left edge of the Confederate line, and the Florida cavalry moving to its left, turning, and setting up defensively at the right edge of the Confederate infantry.

When the Yankee pursuit slowed, the Georgia cavalry moved. They looped to their left, intent on rolling up the unprotected right flank of the federal infantry. Riding in a line perpendicular to the Yankees, the Georgia cavalry should have routed the Union line. Even if the federals had reformed at a right angle to their original line, a charge through the woods by the Confederate 4th Infantry would have broken through and the rout would be on.

This ground had been carefully chosen by General Finnigan. He knew that the marshes to the south, combined with Ocean Pond to the north, narrowed the effective field of maneuver, preventing the Yankee Cavalry from flanking his own Confederate line.

But that same strategy now worked against the Confederates. The pond and marsh kept the Georgia cavalry from swinging deep to the north before turning to charge the Yankees at a right angle. Instead, the Confederate attack had developed at a shallower angle than planned, allowing a longer defensive Union line to brace the attackers. Armed with repeating rifles, a dozen Yankee defenders had the firepower of almost one hundred. As other Yankees hustled to firm up the Yankee right, Mallory's cavalry company had been forced to retreat, and was now back guarding the Confederate left.

And even worse, word had arrived that Colonel Clinch had been wounded in the leg and carried to the rear.

Any flanking effort by the Florida cavalry from the Confederate right would meet a similar fate. If there were to be a breakthrough by either side, it would have to be through a direct frontal assault.

7th Connecticut

Captain Skinner trained his field glasses on the fleeing Georgia cavalry. He had never known a flanking cavalry charge on the raw edge of an unsupported infantry line to fail, and he was proud of the flexibility his regiment had shown in reforming to drive off the rebels.

"Damn!" he said in appreciative wonder to no one in particular.

"Sir?" Lieutenant Dempsey asked.

Captain Skinner swung the glasses to the line of rebels hunkered ahead. The enemy had not coordinated an infantry attack with their cavalry's flanking action. Perhaps they were waiting to see if the Union line crumbled. Or maybe they would have charged if Skinner's whole line had reformed to defend against the cavalry, thereby exposing an unsupported edge in the Connecticut line to the rebel infantry.

The repeating rifles had thwarted the charge. They had not been used by his regiment in combat before, and he hadn't expected so dramatic an effect. Opposite him five rebel regiments were deployed in a thin line. They were supported on both edges by cavalry, but in the thick pines how much of an advantage could horsemen bring? It had gone brilliantly so far, with less than thirty of his men repulsing a full-on cavalry charge, and Captain Skinner felt what the men called battle energy welling up within.

He roughly shoved the field glasses into his waist pouch and grabbed Lieutenant Dempsey and a corporal by their shoulders.

"Spread the word. We advance on my command. Through the woods. Make sure the officers keep the line together. Every man loaded, and we fire as we advance."

As the lieutenant turned to run the captain grabbed him again.

"A constant fire," he barked at both messengers. He pointed at the rebel line opposite, regimental flags still poking from between the pines.

"We attack their center. Drive them back. Have the men reload and fire as targets present. There is no need for controlled fusillades."

He pushed both soldiers off to deliver the order. Sergeants and lieutenants spread the word.

When the messengers returned, Captain Skinner pointed his sword. "Forward!" Again, Skinner was first to step off. He picked up his pace. Firing from his left spread along the line, and soon erupted on his right.

Trees cracked and split above and around the rebel line. Cries of pain carried through the trees from the enemy ranks as the 7th Connecticut poured on firepower as it advanced.

Above his regiment's firing he could hear no sustained rebel return fire. He spotted only sporadic yellow flashes of percussion caps and curling gray smoke above the entrenched enemy line.

And then, he saw something else. As withering fire poured into the rebels, the regimental flags in the middle of their line began to quiver from side to side, and then raise up.

They're moving, he thought to himself. For a moment he believed they were going to charge, but then their flags dropped back. He saw additional chaotic movement in the woods ahead and recognized the first signs of a fall back.

"They're breaking, boys, they're breaking!" Captain Skinner waved his sword over his head in a circle. "After them!"

He quickened his pace.

The Connecticut soldiers poured more fire into the pines. Cries from wounded rebels intensified.

"Keep the line together!" he screamed at his officers.

Some rebels fired before turning and running, and soldiers on both sides of the captain fell.

"On men, on!" he implored. Skinner watched with satisfaction as his men advanced five to ten paces between each of their shots.

Most of the rebels fell back without returning fire. Those who did, didn't reload afterward, but just raced west.

"We've got them on the run, boys! They're breaking, they're breaking! Let's catch them!" Skinner screamed, but the rebel line drew back faster than the Connecticut advance.

"The men are almost out," Lieutenant Dempsey announced.

Skinner turned. His young officer panted hard, his face flushed. He feels it too, the captain thought.

"Order a halt," the captain commanded. "Have the men reload before we continue. Lieutenant, how far do you think we've gone?"

The lieutenant shouted a halt to the advance. Sergeants grabbed the men, commanding them to stop and reload.

Still gasping, the lieutenant turned back to his captain.

"Hard to say for certain, sir. I'd guess, two, maybe three hundred yards."

"The enemy's out of sight," the captain said. "They may still be running. As soon as we reload we'll continue."

"Not quite, sir," Lieutenant Dempsey answered, now studying the terrain in front through his own field glasses. He pointed ahead.

Captain Skinner trained his glasses toward where his junior officer pointed. Through the trees he saw the tip of a Confederate regimental flag. To the right, he spotted another. Neither moved.

"They've stopped and are digging in," the lieutenant said.

"They'll reload," Skinner said. "No matter, we'll do the same and continue on. We'll rout them yet."

More gunfire erupted from their right.

"Another cavalry flank?" Skinner craned his neck to get a better look.

The lieutenant stepped back, angling for a view through the pines. He raised his own glasses.

114

"I don't think so, sir. I think I see another rebel flag on our flank."

"Infantry?" the captain asked.

Rifle fire from the right intensified. Captain Skinner moved to his officer's vantage point. Blue clad soldiers scrambled in the pines to form a defensive line back at a right angle from their original advance.

"What the…?" Skinner asked.

"They didn't fall back, sir."

The lieutenant spun to his left and studied the Union's other flank. He grimaced.

"They didn't fall back. Not all of them. Only the center retreated," the lieutenant repeated.

The captain spun back right again, toward the sound of more rifle fire.

"It's a trap, sir," Lieutenant Seward announced matter-of-factly. "The center moved back, but their regiments on both ends held. They've formed a huge curve and have us surrounded on three sides."

The captain had already stopped listening.

"Get messengers to both flanks," he commanded. "Have the men fall back in a curve to match the rebel curve. We'll form a tight circle within theirs. We'll hold until the New Hampshire 7th catches up and then resume our attack."

"Sir!" a sergeant announced, running in from the left. "It's the men, sir. A lot of the boys just kept firing as they advanced. Especially the new ones. Just stood and fired. They gave no thought to how much ammunition they had. Now they're almost out."

"Damn!" Skinner said. "Still, we should be able to hold. Redistribute what each man has."

"The veteran men aren't going to give up their ammunition," Lieutenant Seward said. "Not to new men who wasted their own."

The captain nodded.

Ducking under branches, a corporal approached the captain.

"The right flank's getting hit hard, sir. The rebs got sharp shooters and a tight target now we're all clumped together. Some of the men are completely out of ammunition."

Through the trees Captain Skinner spotted flashes of sun reflecting off clear metal.

"They're fixing bayonets," he said. "They're preparing to charge."

"Sir, they've got us outnumbered, surrounded on three sides, and we're running low on cartridges," Lieutenant Seward said. "Your orders, sir?"

Skinner swung back to the line in front of him. His soldiers had started their attack with sixty rounds of ammunition each, but sustained firing had expended most of it. Lieutenant Seward was right.

A Confederate flag ahead moved side to side.

Captain Skinner heard a loud yodeling rise from the enemy line.

"A rebel yell, sir," the sergeant said.

"Order the men to fall back!" the captain said. "Get the whole regiment moving, Lieutenant. Have them use what ammunition they have to turn and delay the enemy as we move back. We'll fall back until we meet up with the New Hampshire 7th or the Colored 8th."

A bugler sounded the call to retreat. Men stood and began working their way back through the same trees they had triumphantly advanced between minutes earlier.

Skinner saw the gray line begin to shift as one, readying to pursue his own soldiers. He leveled his revolver at the rebel line. He fired once.

"Make sure the men watch the flanks," he advised. "They'll rush us from the sides too."

"Yes, sir," the young lieutenant answered.

The captain turned and led the race back from the pursuing rebels. This time there was no measured advance.

CHAPTER 19

Last Night

"So, how's it going at the Motel Sex?" Anne asked playfully.

"Close enough," I said. "I'm actually staying at a place called The Dew Drop Inn."

"No way!" she exclaimed. "You've got to be freaking kidding me. Is that really its name? Let me guess, it's across the street from The Aw Shucks, C'mon Inn?"

We both laughed. Breathing a huge sigh of relief, I relaxed the grip on my iPhone. Since applying for the job at the Detroit Free Press I could never be certain how our conversations were going to go. Telling your girlfriend of two years that you're planning to move to a far edge of the country, and leave her behind, can have that effect.

Unable to come up with a clever suggestion to extend the verbal sword play, I changed the topic. "The walls are so thin, I can hear every sound, which is good if you're a journalist."

"And what have you learned through the walls? I mean, other than that marriage vows don't have quite the same import in Northeast Florida."

"Well, apparently, everyone has a marital story about being misunderstood."

"I figured by now you'd be donning a gray wool uniform and complaining about damn Yankees."

"I actually liked that movie."

"No, you liked Gwen Verdon's strip-tease, and the fact that in the end the Yankees lose the pennant."

"*Touché*. Hey, is Cameron in bed?" I tried to sound chipper. "I can say goodnight to her."

I thought I detected a momentary effort to muffle the mouthpiece. When she spoke again Anne's voice had dropped a few degrees in temperature. "She's in bed."

I rolled up on one elbow on the lumpy mattress and held the iPhone away from me to read the digital clock. There was no sense arguing the time. If Anne had decided that I was moving anyway, and she thought it better not to confuse Cameron, well, so be it.

Just when I feared the conversation was about to head south, she switched gears on me.

"So, really, how's it going up there? Getting anywhere with your article?"

Yes! I finally had a chance to prattle and avoid conversational tripwires that could explode into a fight. I launched into my story. But instead of starting with a description of the legislative hearings, I found myself beginning with Agnes Thornberry and the Dunleavys.

She listened in a way that I sensed was more than feigned politeness. It was that passion—for Cameron, for her job, and even for me—that made me fall in love. No wonder she wanted to know more, she'd been a history major before taking the job as a middle school social studies teacher.

She cut into a pause in my story, "Wow, you're getting more than news about cowardly legislators in Tallahassee."

I swallowed and pondered. "Yeah, I guess I am."

Any discomfit over the looming Detroit departure seemed to disappear as I finished my tale.

"You know," she said finally, but still speaking slowly, "I learned about that battle in elementary school. I taught it when I had seventh grade two years ago. It's showcased by many as part of that whole neo-Confederate apologia."

That one I hadn't heard. "Because...?"

"Because the battle need not have been fought."

I scoffed. "You could say that about Vietnam, or Iraq, or—" I started, but she wasn't buying it.

"That's not what I mean," she interrupted. "Those were wars. Even if you subscribe to the Northern version of a justified American Civil War, this particular battle didn't have to happen.

There are those who believe that it wasn't part of any legitimate military strategy. The Union general, what's his name..."

"Seymour," I offered.

"Yeah, that's it. Some believe that Seymour was manipulated into this battle for political and private financial reasons. There's a case to be made that what we today call venture capitalists used their influence to compel him to attack to save their investments. Except back then it wasn't oil as the driving economic force."

"Is this true?" I asked, now sitting bolt upright. "How strong is that evidence?"

"Well, John Hay, one of Lincoln's private secretaries, traveled to see the general shortly before he launched the offensive."

"Really?" Neither Agnes nor the Dunleavys had mentioned this angle.

"There are rumors," Anne continued, "that as reports of the impending offensive reached New York that there was unbridled glee in certain financial quarters..."

Delmonico's Restaurant
2 South William Street
New York City
February 20, 1864
Late afternoon

The waiter placed the steak in front of Marshall Roberts and stepped back. "Will there be anything else, sir?"

Roberts vigorously cut into the meat and lifted his fork for inspection.

"No, that is all for now. But if Mr. Dickerson—Oh! There he is." Roberts motioned toward the restaurant's front door.

The waiter stepped away as Edward Dickerson crossed the room and slid down opposite.

Roberts shook the fork at his companion. "This is absolutely great steak. The rest of the world doesn't know what it's missing.

It could become world famous. I tell you, that Charles Ranhofer fellow is a genius, a verifiable maestro with the carving knife."

"It doesn't have to become world famous," Dickerson said dryly. "They'll make a fortune on what you eat here alone."

Roberts nodded vigorously and dug further into the meat before speaking through a full mouth. "Probably true. But think of it, Dickerson. Here you can order whatever you want off their menu. I get so sick of eating countless business dinners *table d'hôte*."

"Well, now you can have your steak anytime," Dickerson said, studying the plate across which was strewn the already half-consumed meal.

"And a choice of wines." Roberts poured himself a glass. "From a menu just of wines. Speaking of fine eating, and steaks and beef herds, what news do you have?" He wiped his chin vigorously with his napkin.

Dickerson flashed a thin smile and reached into his jacket to extract an envelope.

"Arrived today. Sent up by steamer from Jacksonville. It says Seymour was expected to move west in force in the next few days, by Saturday at the latest. Which, of course, is today."

Marshall Roberts lifted his gold Waltham pocket watch up from its fob and opened it. "So, even as we sit here we may be in the process of getting our railroad back. This, my dear man, is cause for real celebration. See here, Dickerson, order yourself one of these steaks. We'll put it on my tab. Waiter!"

CHAPTER 20

7th New Hampshire

Sergeant Colburn moved to the head of his company leading the 7th New Hampshire Regiment as it marched to the front. The exchange of gunfire told him that the 7th Connecticut was fully engaged. The 7th New Hampshire was to support the attack, but they were far back from a battlefield he still couldn't see.

"Are we winning?" Private Frink asked. The boy licked his lips and swallowed hard.

Instead of resting it on his right shoulder, the lad held the Bridesburg rifled musket with both hands in front of him. He had been issued the new rifle to replace his damaged Springfield. His arms would soon get tired, the sergeant knew, but there was no time to correct him now. Around him, many of the new recruits carried their weapons the same way.

"We'll find out soon enough," the sergeant answered.

They maintained an organized column through the woods. Like the 7th Connecticut, they veered off the road to the right, marching north between the trees. They swung past where the 7th Connecticut was thought to have turned, intending to support the Connecticut men on their right.

But no distances had been given in their orders, and the men of the 7th New Hampshire had lost sight of their Connecticut brethren in the pines. When they heard gunfire coming from the west and slightly behind them, they realized they had swung too far. Colonel Abbott reversed the regiment's march, intent on leading it to a point due east of the gunfire.

Once positioned, Colonel Abbot gave the order to turn once again, and the 7th New Hampshire advanced west toward the sound of battle.

Seven hundred five officers and men of the 7th New Hampshire had set out from Barber Plantation that morning. As Sergeant Colburn encouraged his men to step lively through the trees, he knew that only one-half of Colonel Abbott's regiment held Spencers. The rest had either older Springfields or Bridesburg single-shot rifled muskets. In one company of one hundred men alone, at least twenty-five of those muskets were inoperable, and many had no bayonets.

And of the men who left Barber that morning, more than three hundred were new recruits who lacked both combat experience and proper training. Many spoke French or German, with little or no English.

"Sergeant!" Colonel Abbott called out.

Sergeant Colburn raced forward. The colonel had dismounted and now walked at the head of his column.

"Sir!" The sergeant came alongside his commanding officer. The colonel did not break stride.

"Sergeant, we have no skirmishers in front of us. Select five men and proceed forward. I want to know if—"

Heavier gunfire erupted directly ahead, several single shots followed by a steady staccato. When the colonel stopped, the column halted behind him. Colonel Abbott stared through the trees.

"Where is that coming from, Sergeant?"

Richard Colburn pointed ahead and to the left. "There, sir. Sounded like muskets followed by Spencer carbines."

"Captain Skinner's flank may be under attack. How far do you reckon?" the colonel asked.

The sergeant considered. "A mile. Maybe less. The woods muffle the sound."

More shots followed.

"It has to be a Confederate attack," the colonel said. "Captain Skinner wouldn't attack unless we were there to support."

The colonel turned to his column. "Quicken the pace!"

"We're not heading toward the gunshots, sir?" Sergeant Colburn asked.

The colonel shook his head.

"It sounds like a rebel attack on Skinner's flank. Perhaps skirmishers. If they assaulted his center the gunfire would have been heavier."

"Or an attempted cavalry flank," the sergeant suggested.

The gunfire stopped, and the New Hampshire column picked its way west still not sighting the battlefield.

"Shall I still send out our own skirmishers, Colonel?" Sergeant Colburn asked.

The colonel shook his head. "I think we know where the battlefield is, Sergeant. Captain Skinner must be in front of us."

When the column had advanced an additional fifty yards another staccato of gunfire erupted. Colonel Abbott turned to his sergeant.

"Those are Spencers all right. Skinner's attacking. The 8th must have arrived and is supporting his left."

"On the double quick, men, on the double quick!" the colonel commanded.

Sergeant Colburn led a zigzag pattern through the pines. Although the forest was thick, there was little brush to grab at his legs. Every fifteen or twenty yards he stepped aside to study his men. They followed in a tight column, swerving behind Colonel Abbott.

A blue-clad soldier emerged from the trees in front of them, his rifle swinging wildly in his hands. Colonel Abbott raised his arms and halted the man.

"What's happening?" the colonel demanded.

The soldier leaned over and grabbed his sides, sucking in deep breaths.

"Captain Skinner has called retreat, sir," he huffed. "We advanced on the rebels. Captain had us fire as we went. The middle of the reb line fell back, but their ends held. We only had four companies and they have four, maybe five regiments. Their line formed a horseshoe and we advanced right into the middle of it. We done run out of ammunition and when the rebs started a charge, the captain ordered retreat."

More blue-clad soldiers appeared, racing at full speed. A few stopped and fired back before resuming their run.

"Damnation!" the colonel said.

The groupings of Connecticut soldiers rushing past the New Hampshire column thickened.

Captain Skinner appeared atop a low mound.

"Sir," he said, approaching Colonel Abbott. "The rebels are directly behind us."

Several Connecticut soldiers stopped and started forming up with the New Hampshire regiment, willing to return to a battle with proper support. Captain Skinner moved off and began sorting his own soldiers by pulling them out of line, commanding them to continue to the rear with their own regiment.

A major appeared at Colonel Abbott's side and saluted.

"Orders from brigade, sir," he said. "The rebs are falling back and Colonel Hawley orders your regiment to advance on the run and break their line."

Colonel Abbott pointed in the direction from which Captain Skinner's men fled.

"I don't see rebs falling back, Major," he said. "They charged Captain Skinner and they'll be here any minute. We need to establish a defensive line and hold until the Connecticut 7th is safe behind us, and Colonel Fribley's coloreds can get here."

"These orders are from Colonel Hawley himself, sir," the major argued. "He gave them to me personally to deliver to you."

Sergeant Colburn knew better than to jump into an argument between two officers. There was no way such an action would go well for him. Still…

"Begging the colonel's pardon," he began.

Both officers turned.

"Sir, that was Captain Skinner himself who's now seeing to his men behind us. He would have been the last to leave, sir. And he said there's a rebel advance through these woods. They'll massacre us if we're in column formation. Why, they'd probably be here already if it weren't for these trees."

"This is insolence!" the major erupted. "This is an issue for command, not for a sergeant!"

The major wheeled on Colonel Abbott. "Sir, you have a direct order to advance in a column and deploy to a battle line only when you encounter the enemy. This is directly from Colonel Hawley himself."

The colonel studied the major for several seconds before turning to his sergeant.

"We have our orders, Sergeant. We'll resume the advance."

"Yes, sir," The sergeant turned away. Many of the New Hampshire soldiers sat on the ground, drinking from their canteens.

"On your feet, we're going forward. Come on, let's form up."

The men griped to their feet and reformed. Once the column resumed moving forward, the major stepped off to the rear. When the messenger was out of earshot, Sergeant Colburn turned to his commanding officer.

"Sir," was all he said before a lone straggler from the Connecticut 7th limped into view. His left leg was wrapped, and he used his rifle as a cane.

"They're behind me!" he gasped.

Colonel Abbott climbed atop a tree stump and turned to his regiment.

"Officers!" he yelled. "Get the men in a battle line to the right."

"Sir," a lieutenant protested, "I heard the major give a direct order from our brigade commander to advance."

"I don't care. Men, form on my left!"

Colonel Abbott extended his left arm straight out from his body and pointed to the north. "Do it! Now!"

The men milled about, and the rear of the column bumped into those in front.

Sergeant Colburn grabbed a young private and shoved him roughly to the side. He turned him toward the unseen enemy.

"Here!" he barked. He grabbed another soldier, the recruit he recognized as the Canadian he had tried to train five days earlier and pushed him next to his comrade. Sergeants and officers followed, pushing and tugging soldiers into a make-shift line for which many had never trained. Some veterans raced to take up positions, but many of the new recruits stood about. Some who did follow the commands of the officers got intermingled with soldiers from other companies.

Gunfire exploded from their left. The rebels' first volley cut down the young lieutenant arranging the line. Successive shots tore into the soldiers standing in the column and several fell. The men in the battle line hefted their rifles and waved them wildly, desperate for targets. Sergeant Colburn spotted a line of gray in the trees below a cloud of gun smoke. He jumped to the side of the battle line as a third rebel volley smashed into the Union line.

"Steady, men! Ready!" He raised his arm.

Several soldiers leveled their rifles to their shoulders and pointed them at the gray line.

"Fire!" the sergeant commanded, and half of the makeshift Union line fired at the rebels.

"Back, men! Reload!" he ordered. There had been no time to establish a second line. Now the men tried to reload without cover. Several soldiers dropped their rifles, and others fumbled their ramrods.

To Colburn's left, sergeants and officers shoved soldiers into another battle line, but a fourth rebel volley tore into it.

Two soldiers threw down their rifles and moved behind the nearest pine. Angry screams and cries of pain rang out. The sergeant saw Henry Frink kneeling on the ground, jamming the ramrod down his rifle, seating his next Minié ball. At least someone had followed his training, he thought.

A group of four soldiers from the column moved to the left and fired chaotically at the rebel line. Without sustained volleys, the random shots had little effect.

Another enemy volley erupted from the left. Colburn swore.

Colonel Abbott took over personal command of the Union line that extended to the right. He urged his soldiers to quicken their reloading. Dropped rifles and ramrods littered the ground. Men writhed on pine needles, clutching at seeping wounds. One cried for his mother.

The sergeant monkey-walked to where Colonel Abbott stood, directing counter-fire. He watched as a soldier who had been in the column when the firing began threw down his rifle and raced for the rear.

"Colonel, sir," Colburn said, squatting. "It's no good. The men aren't deployed proper. We're outnumbered and surrounded on three sides. We have no support on our flanks."

Another practiced rebel volley shattered branches and blew bark off the surrounding pines. More Union soldiers fell. Two lay silent.

The soldiers to Colburn's left began backing up, starting their own retreat without orders. Seeing their comrades start to flee, others joined them.

"We need an organized retreat, Colonel, or it'll be a rout."

Another recruit struggling to load his rifle threw it on the ground and broke for the rear. A soldier next to him did the same.

"Colonel," the sergeant implored.

Colonel Abbott stared hard through the pines.

"Men!" he shouted without looking at his sergeant. "Fall back."

He turned to Colburn. "Gather the veterans and cover the rest of the men."

The colonel ran to his left, grabbing and yelling at individual soldiers. Other officers did the same, and by ones and twos the New Hampshire 7th started an organized retreat through the pines.

Sergeant Colburn selected several soldiers and led them forward. All but one had a Spencer repeating rifle. As the rest of the regiment raced for the rear, the sergeant and seven others lay flat on their stomachs and aimed a steady fire at the rebel line. When the sergeant saw that the trees behind him were clear of Union soldiers he raised his arm, and the group rose as one and began their own retreat, turning back and firing every few yards.

When they had moved a safe distance, the sergeant paused and took stock. All seven soldiers he had selected were still with him. The one soldier without a Spencer, who had helped cover the retreat, was Private Henry Frink.

CHAPTER 21

7th Connecticut

Captain Skinner weaved through the trees, searching for stragglers from his regiment. He found them in ones and twos, wandering aimlessly. He pointed them toward where Lieutenant Dempsey was attempting to re-muster the regiment a mile back of the shifting battlefield.

The captain was surprised that his casualties were as light as they were. There had been sustained volleys by both sides, and the air above the battlefield had grown thick with curling smoke, yet most of his soldiers were unscathed. He attributed their good fortune in part to fighting in the woods, where the forest had blocked shots from both sides. And, he reasoned, partly it was because his unit's advance on the rebel center, with its constant barrage, had caught the enemy off guard, initially deterring them from returning volleys until they had fallen back and formed their convex defensive line.

But part of it, he told himself, was that he'd anticipated when the rebels were going to launch their charge with its blood curdling rebel yell and gotten his ammunition-starved regiment back in time to prevent a massacre. If either Abbott's New Hampshire boys, or Fribley's coloreds, had been where they were supposed to be to support his attack, it may have all gone differently.

"Sir."

Captain Skinner scrutinized the exhausted face of Robert Dempsey.

"Yes, Lieutenant?"

"I've rounded up the men we could find. I count two hundred and seventy. More may still be in the woods. Some of the boys were still anxious to fight and didn't want to quit. They turned and joined Abbott's New Hampshire boys as we passed them. So, we appear to be better off than we feared. The men are resting now, but they're itching to go back. That is, if we can get more ammunition."

Around the captain, men squatted on the ground, or leaned back against tree trunks. Dirt streaked soldiers gulped from their canteens, while others checked their weapons. Some moved off to relieve themselves.

"Colonel Hawley himself ordered them to rest on the ground, Captain, when you were off chasing the stragglers."

Captain Skinner nodded absently.

The lieutenant moved in closer. "There might be a problem, sir. In the ranks."

The captain looked at his lieutenant blankly. What else could possibly go wrong?

"Yes?"

"This may not be the time to mention it, but back at the plantation there was a lot of tension among the new recruits. Fights, that sort of thing."

"Go on."

"Well, sir, there was a fight, a knife fight actually, between Privates Dupoy and Rowley, sir."

"I remember. We didn't have time to deal with it then."

"They're both new recruits. If you recall, sir, Private Dupoy cut Private Rowley with his knife. Gashed him up a bit, but the surgeon stitched him back. Dupoy is from Redding. He only enlisted this past November. And Rowley is from Ridgefield. Well, sir, during the fighting today, well, Private Rowley shot Private Dupoy in the head. Killed him, sir."

The captain took a deep breath. This was not something he wanted to hear.

"Intentional, Lieutenant?"

The lieutenant shook his head. "I don't know, sir. Private Rowley says it was an accident, that Dupoy stood up as he fired. But the men, sir. Well, there's grumbling and accusations that it ain't so."

Captain Skinner bit his bottom lip. They might be about to go back into battle and he might have a murderer in his ranks. Just as bad, he might have a soldier who other soldiers thought was a murderer. These incidents had the potential to get out of hand, with the friends of Private Dupoy imposing their own notion of justice during battle. During the next fight anything might happen. And Private Rowley might well have friends who would respond in kind to any effort to meet out justice in the ranks. He'd heard about skirmishes breaking out during a battle between soldiers within the same company.

"We don't have time for this now, Lieutenant."

"Yes, sir."

"Rowley's denied it. I'll conduct a formal inquiry later."

"How far back do you think the ammunition wagons are?" the captain asked, changing the subject.

The lieutenant looked to the southeast and considered. "Not far, sir. When we moved back we may have angled a bit to the north, but the rail bed shouldn't be more than a half mile, one at most."

The captain nodded. "Take some of your strongest men. Get to the rail bed and follow it until you find Colonel Seymour. The ammunition wagons should be with him. We can't get wagons through these woods, and I won't march the men more than I have to. Bring back as much ammunition as you can. We had sixty rounds a man for our last advance, let's try to get one hundred."

A commotion turned the attention of both officers to the west. Blue clad soldiers raced from the trees. A messenger ran up to the officers.

"It's the New Hampshire 7th, sir. They've taken heavy casualties and been pushed back."

4th Georgia Cavalry

Captain Mallory stood next to his mount at the far left of the Confederate line and surveyed the battle. The marshes and Ocean Pond to the north had prevented his cavalry from attempting a second flanking maneuver of the Yankee right.

The captain held his reins loosely, letting his horse nibble the grass in violation of all good training. Let the animal eat, he reasoned. The men in his company did the same. Some tied off their horses and sat on the ground, while others rode forward to serve as skirmishers in the event fortune turned and the Yankees advanced.

So far there was no sign of such. Mallory had seen the Yankees advance piecemeal into battle, units unsupported on their flanks. In addition, the Yankees had advanced in columns, not positioned to return sustained volleys. These mistakes had allowed the undersized Confederate army, even without active cavalry support, to rain fire on their enemy.

A battle designed to be fought from behind the newly constructed earth-works of Camp Beauregard had broken out here instead, and Mallory didn't know why. Confederate units had been sent forward two miles from Camp Beauregard to engage the enemy and, like Mallory's cavalry, lure the Yankees back to the center of the Beauregard fortifications. From that point the Confederates could have engaged the foe from behind a defensive wall.

But General Finnigan had committed more and more troops forward, well in front of the fortifications, until a full-scale battle had broken out in the woods.

There was no returning to the original plan now. Frederick Mallory watched as Colonel George Harrison's brigade arrived from Camp Beauregard and settled in next to Mallory's cavalry company. Soon the whole Confederate Army would be in this forward position. Fellow Georgians, Mallory knew them to be skilled sharpshooters, accustomed to fighting in scattered formations from behind trees and rocks.

The captain sighed and patted his horse. Contrary to plan, the battle had started here, and would be decided here.

CHAPTER 22

8th United States Colored Troops

Private Charles Dunhill was proud that he didn't flinch when he heard gunfire from ahead and to his right. As he studied the faces of the men and officers trudging along the rail bed toward Olustee, it appeared that they too were trying to mask any reaction.

The regiment had never been in battle, but Charles knew no one would admit they were scared. The column of blue marched wordlessly, the dull clank of bayonets against metal the only sound framed by the staccato musketry.

"Must be skirmishers from them Connecticut boys that run to the front," Corporal Cotton said.

The 8th United States Colored Troops had stared transfixed when the Connecticut 7th had double-timed to the lead of Hawley's Brigade. There was a whispered consensus that rebs might be close, and that General Seymour wanted those with the Spencer rifles to meet the enemy first. But since leaving Sanderson, there had been no sign of the enemy.

"Or maybe Henry's Cavalry done run into reb pickets," Charles Dunhill suggested, with what he hoped was an air of authority.

The rifle fire intensified. The caustic booms of cannon split the air.

"That's gotta' be ours," a soldier three rows ahead said.

A succession of response booms from farther away answered, and the column flinched as one at the whoosh of shells overhead.

"Them's reb cannon," another soldier announced unnecessarily.

This was not a skirmish. If cannon were involved, more than pickets or skirmishers lay ahead.

The artillery duel continued, but the rifle fire quieted.

"Mebbe' them rebs is running."

No one laughed. No one answered. The column clanked on.

A mounted rider approached. When Colonel Fribley raised his right hand the column clanked to a halt. Some soldiers dropped the stock of their rifles to the ground and bent over as the messenger reined in. He jumped off his horse and saluted.

"Colonel, sir!" he announced to the 8th's commander, who remained atop his own mount.

"General Seymour wants you to get your regiment to the front with all speed."

The messenger pointed up the railroad bed.

"The 7th Connecticut encountered the enemy in the woods one mile ahead. They've been ordered to capture their battery. You're to support the attack. Set your men to the left of Elder's Horse Battery and protect it and the Connecticut's left flank."

The rate of gunfire picked up again, and then devolved into a steady fusillade.

"Spencers," one soldier announced.

The 8th's second in command, Major Burritt, joined the colonel and the messenger. Charles watched his regiment's senior officers pepper the messenger with questions. The messenger repeatedly shook his head.

Major Burritt yanked two soldiers from the column's front row and sent them racing forward. Each scoured a side of the rail bed as they ran.

The messenger remounted and galloped away.

"Double time!" Colonel Fribley commanded with a raised hand and pointed forward.

Private Dunhill shifted the weight of his back pack and returned his rifle to his right shoulder. The column moved at a quick trot toward the sound of musketry. The gunfire ebbed and flowed, with a steady cacophony interspersed with isolated shots and orchestrated fusillades. The 7th must be under heavy attack, Charles reasoned. His heart pounded, and the icy hand returned to grip his insides.

As the column picked up speed, rifles bounced on soldiers' shoulders. Men grabbed the barrels with their left hands to steady their weapons. A few eschewed a shoulder carry altogether, holding their rifles out in front.

After a half mile the column veered into the woods where one of the advance runners had located a partial path. It was not wide enough for the column, and the soldiers dispersed, searching for pathways.

Charles Dunhill spotted Captain Samuel Elder's Flying Horse Battery set up on a dirt road. Panting heavily from his trot through the woods with full equipment, he studied the artillery operation. The 12-pounder Napoleon cannons of Elder's Battery had been disconnected from their horse teams, which now stood corralled near the ammunition wagons. Men, stripped to their waists, carried projectiles from the limpers stationed to the rear of the cannons up to the big guns.

After each cannon fired, an artilleryman stepped forward and covered the touch hole with his gloved thumb to restrict the air supply to the barrel, while a second swabbed the barrel to remove debris. A third soldier inserted a wet swab, moistened from a water bucket slung beneath the cannon, to extinguish any embers. A burning ember could prematurely explode a shell. When he backed away, a fourth soldier dry-swabbed the barrel to remove moisture. A projectile was inserted into the cannon's mouth, and tamped home with the ramrod. The projectile contained two and a half pounds of powder, a wooden plug, and the cannon shell. The gunner adjusted the height of the cannon and directed its side to side movement before signaling. A long thin pick was inserted into the touch hole to prick open the projectile and expose the gunpowder, quickly replaced by a friction fuse attached to a lanyard. Only then did the crew turn and block their ears as the gunner yanked on the lanyard, causing the fuse to spark, igniting the primer within. The Napoleon exploded in a thunderous convulsion of smoke and flame.

An officer stood with his back to the arriving soldiers, studying the woods through field glasses. Behind him an aide held the reins of two horses. Although the aide cringed with each explosion, and the two horses whinnied and shied, the officer never flinched.

At the sound of arriving soldiers, General Seymour turned.

"Colonel Fribley," he said in a calm voice. "Put your men in immediately."

Grabbing the reins, the general mounted his horse in one motion. His aide scrambled on to his own mount. The general turned and rode off.

"You heard the general," Major Burrit commanded. "Forward."

Following their major, the men swerved around the battery.

Major Burritt led the way toward the battlefield, and the column tucked in close behind.

Charles Dunhill trotted in the middle of a line of soldiers. He craned his neck, trying to spot the enemy. He saw nothing but trees. From ahead he heard the distant shout of "Fire!" followed by an explosion of musketry. Miniè balls ripped into the vegetation around him, and two soldiers to his left collapsed in a heap. He thought one was cowering until he saw the red splotch spread across the man's chest.

"Form two lines, men, two lines!" Lieutenant Norton screamed.

Sergeants began yelling and pushing at the men into two rough lines to face the enemy on their left—one to shoot in unison on command while the other reloaded. But many soldiers did not know in which line to stand, and they crashed into each other as they tried to decide for themselves.

A sergeant, his red sash proudly draped across his torso, stepped to the side and waved his arms and yelled. More shots rang out, and the sergeant crumpled to the ground. A second sergeant did the same and fell clutching at his stomach and screeching.

"Where are they? Where are they?" Corporal Cotton demanded of no one.

Charles Dunhill, rifle still on his shoulder, stepped forward and stared through the trees, searching for the enemy, any enemy. Another volley crashed around him, leaving more men writhing.

"Two hundred yards!" he yelled at the corporal. "They're behind trees, hiding in the dirt!" Charles pointed wildly.

Another rebel salvo inflicted more carnage.

"A line, men! A line!" the lieutenant screamed, and Charles stepped into a line facing left. There were about twenty men with him, most of the other soldiers choosing to stand as the second line.

"Ready, aim!" Lieutenant Norton commanded.

Charles un-shouldered his rifle and pointed it at the rebels in the trees. He realized he had never loaded his weapon.

He considered stepping back to load his Springfield, but worried that doing so would reveal that he had walked into his first battle with an unloaded rifle. Better to pretend to fire the first volley and then step back as if reloading.

When other soldiers lowered their own rifles before the command to fire came, he realized that no one in the makeshift line had loaded their weapon.

"Shall we load our rifles?" one soldier asked.

The lieutenant stared back, dumbfounded.

Another volley ripped into the men. One soldier stared down at his friend lying next to him, the top of his head missing. He began to shake, and then cry, before falling to the ground, cupping his own head in both hands. He curled into a ball.

Charles dropped to the ground and scrambled to where Colonel Fribley was setting up another line to the right. He spotted a line of gray dug into the earth two hundred yards in front of him.

There was no longer any pretext of organized lines. The soldiers of the 8th United States Colored Troops were scattered in the dirt and pine needles, intermingled with the dead and dying. Charles couldn't tell who was injured, and who cowered. He searched for guidance, but Colonel Fribley moved off and squatted on the ground, consulting with the major. To his left, Lieutenant Norton still screamed orders. Almost all the sergeants now lay dead or bleeding, their blood indistinguishable from their red sashes.

Charles rose to his knees and tried to acquire a target in the scooped-out earth less than 200 yards away. He couldn't find a clean one, but took the best shot he had. He had no idea if he hit anything.

Throwing himself back on the ground he reloaded and rolled over taking another shot. Other soldiers, recovered from the initial onslaught, and individual soldiers of the 8th, returned scattered fire.

Colonel Fribley crawled to Charles Dunhill.

"Fall back!" He turned, facing the men. "Reform at the cannons!"

Few soldiers moved.

"Get them back, Private," the colonel ordered, before crawling to the next group of soldiers hunkered in the dirt.

Charles waited until the colonel had moved away before standing.

"Everyone!" he yelled. "The colonel has ordered us to fall back."

He crouch-walked backwards. Several soldiers joined him as heavier fire erupted from the Confederate lines.

Major Burritt stood at the rear of the regiment, grabbing men as they passed and pushing them along to the rear.

"Fire as you move back," he instructed.

Charles moved back through the pines, turning, firing and reloading every twenty yards. The regiment retreated slowly. It did not break and run.

Colonel Fribley stood in the open, surveying the retreat he had ordered. He clasped at his chest and slumped to the ground. Charles raced to him, arriving at the same time as Corporal Cotton. The colonel looked at the private with eyes already flickering.

"Now take me away," the colonel said. He closed his eyes and went limp.

Major Burritt dropped down alongside. Charles Dunhill and Thomas Cotton knelt over the lifeless form of their commanding officer. Corporal Cotton cradled his head.

"The colonel's dead, sir," the corporal announced.

Major Burritt nodded. "Keep moving back." He crawled over to another huddled group of soldiers.

Charles and Thomas reloaded and stood. They waited for more soldiers to pass to get a clear field of vision. They fired before again moving back.

Forty yards to the rear another soldier raced up.

"It's Major Burritt." The soldier's face had turned ashen white. "He's shot up real bad. Both legs gone. He can't talk none."

"Where is he?" Thomas Cotton looked, scouring the woods.

"Two men carried him," the soldier answered. "But I don't think he's going to make it. His legs are gone."

Charles swallowed hard.

"There ain't nobody in command, now, nobody," the soldier wailed. Other soldiers took up the refrain.

Corporal Cotton grabbed the young soldier by the shoulders. "Steady, boy." He shook him roughly. "Lieutenant Norton is still in command."

"Look! There're the cannons!" Charles said, pointing. "That's battery M of the First Artillery. We almost there. They'll protect us."

Corporal Cotton waved encouragement to his fellow soldiers stumbling back through the woods.

"We can get a line here," he said.

The soldiers moved behind the cannons, as if to use the guns and caissons as cover. Other soldiers huddled in groups of from two to ten. Some still held rifles, many did not.

Rebel fire poured in from the left and from in front, targeting the larger groups huddled together. From two hundred fifty yards, a tight group presented a large target. Union soldiers began scooping out their own rifle pits, while others lay in the dirt returning individual sporadic fire.

Corporal Cotton ran to the captain in command of the cannons.

"Can you drive these rebels off?"

Charles Dunhill joined them.

The captain's face was streaked by sweat, dirt and traces of blood. He panted heavily.

"I can't drive what I can't see. We only have the rebel gun smoke to guide us. I can't see them."

"They're out there," Charles said.

The captain pointed to where two artillerymen lay sprawled in the dirt, dead. "Oh, they're out there, Private. But I still can't see them. And when I move my battery one way or another, the trees get too thick and we can't fire, let alone see them."

"I see them," Corporal Cotton said, pointing to the right. "They're coming."

The captain swore. He leaped to the cannons with his remaining crewmen, and together they spun the Napoleon to the right where movement in the grass betrayed the enemy advance.

"Grape!" he screamed. "Grape!" and his crew loaded the cannon. They had only begun to step away when the captain yanked the lanyard. The rustling grass exploded in a plume of smoke and dust, and all movement ceased.

The 8th's surgeon, Dr. Alex Heichold, crawled among the wounded, directing the loading of soldiers into his horse-drawn ambulance.

"Help me," he implored any infantrymen or artillerymen who remained standing. "We need to get the wounded out of here. I know what will become of the white troops who fall into the enemy's possession, but I'm not certain as to the fate of our coloreds."

CHAPTER 23

February 20, 1864
Late afternoon
General Alfred Colquitt's Command

Captain Mallory had never seen General Colquitt this angry.

"I think the fight's going well, sir," the captain offered.

"We need to capture that battery," the general spluttered, waving his arm toward the sound of Union cannons without looking up from the field maps spread across the makeshift table before him.

Having been summoned back to the general's command. Captain Mallory still expected a role for the cavalry. He waited patiently.

"How's Colonel Clinch?" the general asked.

"He was carried from the battlefield. A wound to his leg. I don't know how serious."

The general continued to stare at the maps, and Mallory wondered how interested he was in the answer.

"It's those damn niggers." General Colquitt folded over a map and looked up. "We hit them good as they came on the field. Never even set up. They should have broke and run, and we'd have those damn Yankee cannons. But they fell back and aren't quitting. They're not set up proper, but between their fire and the cannons we can't approach. If we can take the cannons we can rout the whole Union Army, drive them all the way back, maybe even retake Jacksonville."

The captain said nothing.

"I've ordered the 19th and 28th Georgia Infantry to keep pressure on the cannons and the Yankee infantry. They advance, but then the damn cannons and nigger firing drives them back. I'm sending the 6th Florida Battalion to swing around and attack from the south. In the cross-fire the Yankee line should break."

The general spun to the captain. "The right flank of the 6th Florida will be exposed to Yankee Cavalry. That's Henry's Union Cavalry out there, and when they realize we've swung around their niggers and attacking from the side, Henry may send one or two companies to attack our own edge. I need you to keep Henry's Cavalry off the Florida 6th."

"Yes, sir."

"That's Hawley's Union Brigade out there we're dealing with, Captain. It has three regiments, and if we get these niggers on the run their whole brigade will be smashed. And Hawley's Brigade is the best Seymour has."

He moved closer to the captain.

"If we get them on the run, General Seymour may try to get another of his brigades to attack, but by then we'll have brought up seven regiments and a battalion, and we'll be deployed in a well-formed line. We'll have nearly four hundred and fifty cavalry. I'll have maybe four thousand five hundred men. We'll break through.

"And when we do, Captain, I want you to stay on the battlefield. Chase the enemy when they break, harass them all the way to Jacksonville, keeping up constant contact. Do not let them rest."

The captain saluted, turned and walked to his mount. It was a short distance to where his company rested among the pines, and the ride gave him an opportunity to reflect.

General Finnigan was supposedly in charge. General Colquitt had arrived from Georgia to assist, but it appeared to Mallory that Colquitt was in charge. The general had referred on multiple occasions to the strength that he, not the Confederate Army, would have. Mallory could only hope that General Finnigan had acquiesced to this change. If not, trouble could lie ahead.

Mallory's cavalry company mounted and swung behind the Confederate command before turning and heading south. After two miles they turned east, intending to take a position to the right of the Florida 6th to protect the Floridians' flank. But as they passed south of the 6th, Mallory heard gunfire to his left. The Floridians had already begun their attack on the Negroes' flank without waiting for the cavalry to arrive.

Mallory shook his head. The Yankees had made many dumb moves this day that allowed the Confederates to gain a tactical advantage, but the Confederates were making their own share as well.

Quickening his gait, Mallory led his company left, coming up on the right flank of the Florida 6th Infantry Battalion. To his relief, Colonel Henry's Union cavalry had not counter-attacked. Mallory deployed his cavalry in a defensive line to await a possible Union cavalry attack.

It never came.

Instead, Frederick Mallory watched as the 6th Florida Infantry laid down a devastating cross fire on the Negro infantry regiment and artillerymen still manning their Napoleons. Now facing fire from two directions, the Negroes disengaged, pulling further back to the east. The artillerymen tried to take their cannons with them, but most of the Union horses were dead. A few soldiers rolled cannons by hand. The Negroes laid down masking fire as they retreated with the artillerymen, allowing their regiment and some cannons to escape.

Captain Mallory held his position until a soldier from the 6th Florida waved at him.

"They've broken, sir!" he called out triumphantly. "We've captured five big guns the Yankees left behind, and they're running back to the ocean."

* * *

Captain Skinner sat cross-legged on the ground and watched as stragglers from the 8th United States Colored Troops and artillerymen, some pushing cannons wobbling on two-wheeled carriages, approached down the dirt road toward where the Connecticut 7th rested among the trees.

He knew the coloreds had had a bad go. Some walked singularly, a stony, open-mouthed expression on their faces. Others supported limping comrades. Several covered bloody wounds with makeshift bandages.

The surgeons directed the wounded to one of two areas. In the first, the doctors stood ready, grisly tools in their hands. In the other, field medics sat the men down and tried to make them comfortable. Already sheets covered a pile of bodies. Captain Benjamin F. Skinner looked away.

It didn't have to have been like this. If Colonel Henry's cavalry, with their own repeating rifles, had joined his assault, or if Abbott's New Hampshire men or the 8th Regiment had been in position as he had been told they would be, the outcome might have been different. The 7th Connecticut was only four companies, but their repeating rifles could have been enough if there had been support for their attack.

"Sir!"

It was Lieutenant Dempsey.

"Sir, the men have been given ammunition. They'll be carrying one hundred rounds this time, some more."

The captain looked up. "This time?"

"Yes, sir. General Seymour has ordered Barton's New York Brigade to join the fight. We're to gather uninjured from the coloreds and support the New Yorkers on their left."

Captain Skinner studied the trail clogged with stragglers.

"The New Yorkers?" he asked.

"Yes, sir. Barton has the 47th, 48th and 115th New York Infantry regiments. And this time we'll advance in battle line, ready for the rebs, not in a damn fool column. And we've still got the Massachusetts 54th and the North Carolina First Colored Volunteers."

"The North Carolina First has never been in battle," Skinner said absently. He watched as another cannon rolled into view pushed by four soldiers, one of whom was wrapped in red bandages. As it entered the clearing its right wheel fell off. The soldiers swore, and one of the four kicked at it.

"No, sir, but the 54th can fight. And Barton's Boys are good."

"Why is the 8th joining us as individual soldiers?" Skinner asked, turning back to his junior officer. "Are they that bad off?"

Lieutenant Dempsey lowered his voice.

"Sir, they've done some counting. Of the 575 men the 8th Colored had this morning, over half are dead or wounded. Every one of their sergeants is dead. They say the sergeants never got their sashes off before they were in the thick of it, and reb sharpshooters got everyone."

"What about their officers?" Skinner asked. "Aren't they coming too? They can still command whoever is left."

The lieutenant was already shaking his head.

"Sir, Colonel Fribley is dead. The second in command, Major Burritt, is shot up bad and not expected to live. Sir, of the twenty-three officers they had this morning, only two aren't dead or injured."

The captain stood up and tugged on his cap.

"Round up the men, Lieutenant, and get who you can from the coloreds. We're advancing to the battlefield."

CHAPTER 24

February 20, 1864
Late afternoon

Lieutenant Norton squatted in the dirt and clasped Charles Dunhill by the shoulder.

"How you men doing?"

Splayed on the ground next to Charles, Corporal Cotton looked up. He was adjusting the hammer hinge on his Springfield by forcing his bayonet under it.

"We're alive, Lieutenant."

"And you, Private?" the lieutenant asked, directing his attention to Charles.

Charles swallowed and nodded. "We thank the Lord we alive."

The lieutenant patted the private's shoulder. "We never got a chance to set a proper battle line. It could have been different. But you two did well. Real well."

"The colonel's dead, sir," Corporal Cotton said. "I been with him when he died."

"I know, Corporal."

"The sergeants are gone," Corporal Cotton added. "Every one of them."

"Major Burritt, sir?" Charles asked. "Is he still alive?"

The lieutenant shook his head. "I don't know."

"Now what happens, sir?" The corporal searched the grass littered with soldiers of the 8th. "What now?"

"We're going back."

"Back, sir?" Charles asked. "To the battle? Or you mean Jacksonville?"

The lieutenant stood. "General Seymour has ordered Barton's New Yorkers forward. The Connecticut 7th will support their left. They took a pounding today, too. Those of us who aren't wounded are to move up with them."

"As part of the 7th?" Charles asked. "We now part of them?"

"Yes and no. We're no longer a full regiment, and our commanding officer and second are both gone. But we have soldiers who can fight. We'll be part of the 7th, but will form up on their left, the extreme left end of the Union line."

The lieutenant studied the field. "What officers we have will direct fire. You men load up on ammunition, we're going forward."

The lieutenant moved off.

"Another chance at them rebs," Corporal Cotton said. "'Cept this time we be ready."

Men moved in twos and threes back to where other soldiers handed out paper cartridges and percussion caps from crates in the back of a supply wagon. Each soldier filled his ammunition pouch to the top, and then grabbed extra rounds for his pockets before wandering to a nearby stream to fill his canteen.

When they returned, they started to form up in a column for the march back toward the gunfire.

"No column, men," the lieutenant barked. "We're going to walk through these woods shoulder to shoulder with the Connecticut 7th. We'll form the battle line here. When we get to where the fighting is, we're going to be ready."

Together with the men of the Connecticut 7th and 8th, they stepped off through the woods. Moving in front of the line and raising his arms, Lieutenant Norton slowed the men of the 8th until they lagged behind their Connecticut brethren. Starting at the far-left-end of the line, he worked his way to the right, designating every other man as part of a second line.

When he finished, he moved again to the front, turned, and walking backwards, addressed the remaining soldiers of the 8th United States Colored Troops.

"When we get back to the battlefield I want those I put in line one to step forward and fire a volley on my command, or the command of an officer from the Connecticut boys. After firing I want line one to step back and reload. I want line two to step forward and take their place. We will fight this way all afternoon and all night if we need to. Do you understand?"

Several soldiers shouted, "Yes, sir!"

"Good," the lieutenant continued. "I want everyone to load now. We're going to enter the battle loaded and ready to kill rebels."

Charles Dunhill reached into his pouch and pulled out a cartridge and percussion cap. He loaded his rifle without stopping his march. Lieutenant Norton walked up and down the line offering assistance and correction where needed.

"Let's show those rebel traitors the 8th knows how to fight!" the lieutenant yelled. There was another resounding crescendo of "Yes, sir!"

The lieutenant resumed his place at the front of the extended line. Rifles now held out in front, the men of the 8th quickened their pace and caught up shoulder to shoulder with the Connecticut 7th.

"How many you think we got?" Corporal Cotton asked no one in particular.

"I heard Colonel Barton got about fifteen hundred New York white boys," a soldier to Charles Dunhill's right answered. "And they been in plenty of scraps."

"When we was lining up I counted the Connecticut boys and us. We got maybe five hundred altogether," another answered.

"How many the rebs got?" a third soldier asked.

"I don't know," Corporal Cotton said. "But they got more now than when they sleep tonight."

"Lord's truth!" Several soldiers nodded encouragment.

The sound of gunfire intensified. Charles spotted a Confederate regimental flag two hundred yards ahead. From the start of the battle hours earlier until now, he estimated that the Union line had been pushed back two miles.

Shouts of "There they are!" rang out up and down the Union line.

"Line one!" the lieutenant shouted, and the designated soldiers stepped forward, rifles raised. Line two remained back five yards. To his right, Charles Dunhill watched the men of the Connecticut 7th do the same.

"Fire!" a Connecticut sergeant called out, and the line to Charles' right exploded in a swath of flame and smoke that curled upward.

"Fire!" Lieutenant Norton screamed. Charles was already moving back as the second line took up the forward position. But before the second line could fire, a return volley from across the battlefield tore into it. Three soldiers fell. Two clutched at wounds. The third lay still.

As Charles worked his ramrod, soldiers in line two bent to help their fallen comrades.

"Leave them!" Norton barked. "Keep the line. We must keep a line of fire. Ready!"

As Charles reloaded he saw soldiers from the Connecticut regiment fall, and heard their officers shouting the same command not to break line to help the fallen. The officers must have been told this before they rejoined the battle, he reasoned. It would be different this time, it would be a fight to the end, with no quarter given.

Charles placed a percussion cap on his rifle's nipple. Line two stepped back. He was at the fore again, his rifle raised and leveled. The lieutenant waited for line two to begin its own reloading process. Dunhill sited down his rifle, searching for a target. The rebs had spread out, firing from the cover of trees and the conceal of deep grass.

"Fire!" the lieutenant barked. Charles stepped back without seeing what he'd hit.

To his far right, the New Yorkers kept up a barrage. Both sides traded continuous volleys, and the ground filled with fallen soldiers.

When a young soldier asked to be allowed to go back and pee, Lieutenant Norton responded with, "In your trousers, Private."

Some soldiers chugged water after firing, racing to catch up with their line's reloading. As the afternoon wore on the rigid firing lines deteriorated, and Union soldiers began adopting the strategy of their Confederate foes, leaning out to fire from behind pines. The firing on both sides became ragged. The firing commands were useless as soldiers reloaded and fired as soon as they thought they saw a target.

The Confederate line was longer than the Union's, and Charles watched as its right edge began snaking its way through the trees to his left. He remembered what happened hours earlier.

Choking gun smoke filled the air, and he found it difficult to acquire targets through the enveloping fog. Sometimes he fired at a flash. As the sun began to set, the effect of the haze intensified, until little could be seen through the trees.

The Confederates kept angling to the Union left. To his right, Charles saw the Connecticut 7th start to creep back, and further along, the left edge of Barton's New York Brigade did the same. The order soon came to the 8th, and they too edged back, trying to remain even with the Union lines to their right.

With coordinated firing all but abandoned, Lieutenant Norton moved among the troops, offering support and encouragement.

"How you fixed?" he asked Charles.

"Almost out, sir. Maybe ten rounds left. Not a good time with them rebs trying to move around us."

"That's the 6th Florida Battalion trying to loop around," the lieutenant answered. "Them's the ones that flanked us last time. But this time we got Massachusetts Cavalry to protect our flank. That's Stevens himself. I don't think he'll let them get around."

"Won't matter much if we run out of cartridges."

Corporal Cotton joined the pair, leaning against a tree with his back to the enemy.

"A lot of the boys are almost out," he said. "I told them to slow their firing, make it last. We keep moving back, keeping them rebs in front of us, but they got too many along their line."

He pointed toward the Union right. "It looks like the 47th New York is backing up. They must be running low. This could get bad if they turn and run."

Lieutenant Norton studied the fog at the far side of the battlefield. "Did you notice the rebel fire dying down?"

Both soldiers craned their necks and squinted.

"They're running out too," Corporal Cotton said gleefully. "Lordy!"

"Look!" Charles said. Across the field a rebel officer in a general's uniform rode along the line, tossing small bags to clumps of men who stretched out their arms to catch them.

"Things must be bad over there too if they got themselves a general running messenger errands, delivering ammunition."

The Connecticut 7th began moving back faster, a formal skirmishing line set up behind their withdrawal. The Connecticut skirmishers turned and followed at a safe distance, firing volleys to cover their unit's retreat in the event the rebs charged. There was no sign of such a movement from the Confederate side.

"Them Spencer rifles are sure nice enough firing, but they don't last long before the Connecticut boys run through all their cartridges that way," Corporal Cotton said.

A messenger found Lieutenant Norton.

"Sir, it'll be dark soon," he said, studying the sky. "You're ordered to take your men to the rear. We're out of ammunition across the whole line. The 54th will take your place and cover your retreat. The First North Carolina Colored Volunteer Regiment will cover the right. They'll fight a delaying action. The general wants to try and make Barber Plantation tonight."

CHAPTER 25

February 20, 1864
Dusk
54th Massachusetts Volunteer Infantry

For the men of the 8th United States Colored Troops, the walk back from the battlefield to the Union's staging area was nothing like their earlier one. The regiment had entered the day without battle experience, and devoid of adequate training in either deployment or weapons handling. They had marched onto the battlefield against an experienced Confederate foe, and the result was unsurprising. After recovering to fight bravely, if ineffectively, they retreated in shambles, their corps of officers and sergeants destroyed, their ranks decimated by Confederate shot.

Now they left the field as a battle-tested unit. Their stride reflected their new-found achievement. They lined up as a unit as they departed, and marched to the rear with regimental colors flying, many of the men singing the same patriotic songs they had sung when they left Barber Plantation that morning.

A mile and a half to the rear they encountered the 54th Massachusetts Volunteer Infantry marching west to replace them. Having been authorized as a state militia by order of Massachusetts Governor John Andrew in March 1863, after the Emancipation Proclamation, but prior to the Union Army's official decision in May 1863 to enlist black troops, the 54th Massachusetts did not carry the name "Colored" in its designation as the federal regiments did.

When its formation was announced, efforts by freed blacks to enlist in Massachusetts was so strong that only the most able and fit were selected, giving the unit a robust air lacking in other units, white or black. The interest remained strong despite the proclamation by Confederate President Jefferson Davis on December 23, 1862 that the Union's efforts to use black soldiers amounted to servile insurrection, and that any black soldiers caught were subject to immediate execution on the battlefield, and their white officers hung. That proclamation had been confirmed by the Confederate Congress the following January.

Ever since their heroic efforts the previous July, the 54th had enjoyed a storied reputation across the North and throughout the Union Army. At Barber Plantation the men of the 8th United States Colored Troops had gawked whenever encountering soldiers from the Massachusetts regiment.

But now, as the battle weary 8th marched back, Colonel Edward Hallowell stopped his 54th, and their ranks parted to allow the men of the 8th to pass. The soldiers of the 54th removed their caps and gave one rousing huzzah after another to their black brethren.

"Look's like we done arrived," Corporal Cotton whispered in awe to Charles as they marched between the cheering ranks.

After the 8th passed, the 54th reformed and resumed its trek toward the battlefield. Off to the side, Lieutenant Norton, now missing his cap, conferred with an officer from the Connecticut 7th.

"Don't seem right, they gonna' finish this without us, does it?" Charles asked his corporal.

"I mean, we been fighting all day, up to the battle twice, and now we finally know how to beat them rebs, and the 54th gonna' get all the glory again?"

"What you thinkin' boy?" Corporal Cotton rubbed the back of his aching neck.

Lieutenant Norton finished his conversation with the Connecticut officer and turned back to his own regiment.

"Sir!" Private Charles Dunhill stepped abreast of Norton. The lieutenant paused.

"Sir, you said the 8th was no longer a proper regiment right now, and that's why us soldiers fought with them Connecticut boys. Sir, I would like to join with the Massachusetts 54th and go back and finish this day with them."

Hearing Charles, other soldiers from the 8th joined in the request.

Corporal Cotton lowered his rifle. "I won't let you boys go it alone. I'd like to go too, sir."

Lieutenant Norton looked at the rear of the 54th column, now fifty yards up the trail. He turned to the group of five soldiers surrounding him.

"All right. How you boys fixed for ammunition?"

"Not much, sir," one replied.

"Take some from the wounded at the end of our column. Run and join the 54th. Tell an officer I gave you permission to do this."

Grabbing what cartridges and caps they could scrounge, the five soldiers raced after the 54th. When they caught up they told a soldier what they were intending. He signaled to an officer, and the five repeated their desire to fight with the Massachusetts regiment. The officer positioned them at the rear of the column.

A mile from the battlefield, Colonel Hallowell signaled a halt. The sounds of battle were directly ahead. General Seymour and two aides sat atop their horses at the side of the trail. As the 54th clanked to a stop the general walked his mount directly to Colonel Hallowell and stood up in his stirrups. When he spoke, he addressed not only the commanding officer, but the whole regiment.

"Men," he said, "the battle is lost. Everything depends on the 54th."

He lowered himself back down in his saddle and spoke to the colonel.

"Form your men on the left of the Union line. The Connecticut 7th and the 8th Colored have already moved to the rear. The First North Carolina Colored Volunteers will form on the right of the Union line. You are to support the Union line for as long as practicable. Then the New Yorkers will be able to retreat from the middle when they are out of ammunition. I want your regiment and the First North Carolina to cover the withdrawal of Barton's Brigade.

"Colonel, you are outnumbered by the enemy," the general continued, "but we need at least a half hour head start if we're to save this army and get it back to Jacksonville. Can you hold for that long?"

Instead of answering his commanding officer, Colonel Hallowell committed military insolence by himself standing tall in his stirrups and twisting around to face his regiment.

"You heard the general. Can we hold that long?"

The answer from the ranks was a unanimous cheer.

"Then let us lighten our weight and rush to the enemy!" Hallowell exclaimed.

The soldiers of the 54th immediately removed their knapsacks, haversacks filled with food rations, and blankets, and threw them to the side of the road before reforming their column. Colonel Hallowell saluted the general and dug his spurs into his horse's sides, taking off at a trot. The men of the 54th broke into a run after him.

"They know what they're doing," Charles said.

The 54th ran the last mile to the battlefield, the sounds of battle growing louder at each turn. As they twisted through the woods they spotted the ragged left edge of the 47th New York. The remnants of Barton's Brigade moved back through the trees, occasionally turning and firing. When the men of the 47th spotted their reinforcements, they turned and cheered.

"Battle line!" Colonel Hallowell shouted, and the officers directed the establishment of two lines. The five soldiers from the 8th stood together in the front. When an officer gave the command to fire they unleashed their salvo and stepped back to reload with the rest of their line. But to Charles' surprise the men of the 54th never undid the ramrods slung beneath their rifles. Instead, eschewing accepted manual of arms, the soldiers ripped open the powder cartridges with their teeth, poured the contents down the barrels of their rifles and dropped the Minié ball on top, and then tapped the butts of their rifles on the ground to knock the Minié ball to the bottom. While Charles fumbled with his own ramrod, his line was already back in firing position and delivering another salvo.

Using their unorthodox reloading method, the 54th kept up a withering rate of fire. The Confederates, who had been inching their way forward, broke off their advance. After ten volleys by both lines Charles noted the Confederates' return fire slacken, and he spotted the enemy moving back.

"It's the New Yorkers, sir!" a panting white officer who had crossed the field said to the colonel. "They're out of ammunition and leaving the battle."

Colonel Hallowell acknowledged with a wordless salute.

The 54th continued to pour it on. As the Confederates got pushed back, the 54th moved forward and to the right to block the enemy from charging the gap left by the retreating New Yorkers.

But the 54th also repositioned cautiously. They were not going to repeat the mistake the Connecticut 7th had earlier that day.

The sun set, and still the 54th poured it on. Only when a messenger informed Colonel Edward Hallowell that the First North Carolina Colored Volunteers were also pulling back did the colonel order his unit to cease fire.

A stillness enveloped the forest. The odor of gunpowder hung heavy. Charles squinted through the haze and fog of war at the enemy across the battlefield. Rebel regimental flags were no longer in view. The return fire was sporadic. The cries of men in pain echoed from all corners.

"We're moving back," the colonel announced. "The North Carolina First held for over an hour and a half. That'll give Barton's Brigade a huge head start, if the rebs even want to try and pursue at night." He studied the darkening sky. "Let's move out."

But the soldiers who had moved so seamlessly all day refused to readily leave the battlefield. The men of the 54th lingered, not firing their muskets, but standing with arms folded across their chests, posturing toward an enemy hunkered less than three hundred yards away.

"Sometimes, war gets personal," Charles said in a low voice.

Corporal Cotton turned to him. "You have no idea," the former slave said.

"You're wrong," Charles answered. "I do."

The pair rejoined their own battle line, which turned and moved back. The wounded who could walk were given a head start, followed by those who needed assistance. The unscathed soldiers reloaded and followed in a battle line as they picked their way back through the forest. Occasionally the line turned and fired a salvo to keep the rebels at bay. Only isolated shots were returned. If the enemy was pursuing, it did so half-heartedly.

"You think today will count as one battle or three?" Corporal Cotton asked, after firing a covering shot.

Before he could answer, Charles pitched forward to the ground. He thought he must have tripped on a branch, until he felt the sharp pain in his right hip, just below his belt.

"Damn!" He pulled himself over onto his back.

Two soldiers from the 54th bent to look at his leg.

"What is it?" Charles asked.

"You been hit," one of the soldiers answered as he yanked a knife from his belt. He sawed at the uniform's pant leg.

"It don't feel bad. It just—" Charles began, but the wave of pain shooting down his leg made him wince.

"Can you walk?" another soldier asked.

The rest of the battle line didn't stop but kept moving back and reloading. Charles thought of Lieutenant Norton not allowing the men of the 8th to break line to help fallen comrades. What had happened to them? What would happen to him? Would the soldiers of the 54th who had bent down to help leave him? Would the corporal? He'd only known Thomas Cotton a few months. Was that enough time for him to stay behind to help?

The 54th's battle line faded into the trees. A soldier shoved a rag on the wound, and a second added the kerchief from his neck.

"You gotta' try," the soldier repeated. "You can't stay here."

Together with Corporal Cotton they lifted Charles to his feet.

"Can you put weight on it?" one asked.

He tried. It wasn't the pain, but he seemed to have lost strength in his right leg.

"One man," one of the soldiers said, and the two soldiers from the 54th looked at each other.

"I'll take him," Thomas Cotton said, and moved to Charles' right side. He placed the private's right arm over his shoulder and leaned in to take the weight. Charles held his rifle in his left hand.

"Leave it," one of the soldiers said.

Charles tossed his rifle aside.

"And the belt too," the soldier added. "You don't need extra weight."

Thomas Cotton undid Charles' belt and dropped the ammunition pouch to the ground.

"I'll be fine," Corporal Cotton said, and the two soldiers of the 54th turned and ran after their own retreating skirmish line without another word.

Charles put one foot in front of the other, stepping with his left and swinging his right. With his rifle tossed aside, he tried to keep the bandage in place on his right hip by crossing his left hand and pressing it tight against the wound.

The Union skirmish line was soon out of sight. Charles swung his right foot as fast as he could, hoping to see the line reappear.

"How far to where we set up?" Charles asked after awhile. "We should be there by now, shouldn't we?"

"There ain't no more base in the woods." Thomas Cotton glanced at Charles. "The whole damn Union Army done moved back to Jacksonville by now if they could have, leastways Barber Plantation by morning. We got to keep up 'cause there ain't gonna' be no help 'til we meet up with them."

"I can't go that far."

"I don't want to hear nothing noble about me leaving you." Thomas held tight to Charles. "There's a reason I'm your corporal. I don't know if them rebs be following, but if so, we can't stop, least, not until we reach Sanderson."

CHAPTER 26

This morning
Olustee Battlefield Historic State Park

The forecast rain hadn't started, but the clouds hung gray and low and a southern breeze had whipped up, driving a styrofoam cup across the parking lot in front of my car. I swung around a parked Malibu with South Carolina plates and pulled into the same spot I had the day I met Agnes Thornberry. This time there were several other cars in the lot—none with Florida plates.

Olustee Battlefield State Historical Park is a mesh of state and federal land. In 1909, the State of Florida purchased three acres and constructed a historical monument. Three years later, when Civil War veterans still attended reunions, the acreage became Florida's first historic site. In 1949, it became its first state park.

Although owning only the three original acres, Florida managed the surrounding 688 acres of the battlefield under a special use permit from the National Forest Service. Bill told me there was a one-mile trail with interpretive signs that wound through the forest, following the battle lines. Since the terrain was essentially unchanged in the last 150-plus years, I figured it was a good idea to see for myself where Frederick Mallory, Alfred Colquitt and Charles Dunhill had stood and fought.

The Chevy's two passengers remained inside as I locked my BMW. I assumed they must have finished their own tour and were preparing to leave when their front doors swung open, the passenger side one nearly crunching my fender. Two women who looked to be in their early sixties got out.

"Don't worry, it's an older model," I said when the shorter one shot me an apologetic look.

"I'm always telling Caroline to be careful with her door," the driver scolded. "But she never listens."

Walking behind their car I noticed the rear bumper sticker: "If At First You Don't Secede, Try, Try Again."

Maybe this would be the story I had hoped to get from Agnes Thornberry.

"Taking the trail?" I asked, intent on joining them.

I am always amazed at what a talisman identifying myself as a journalist is to wheedle conversation. I resolved that if I ever became a serial killer I'd retain the journalism cover.

I kept the conversation light, hoping to get as much background as possible. They were sisters from Charleston who'd retired from teaching the driver, Mabel, told me. Together with their husbands—also retired—they snow-birded in The Villages retirement community, an hour north of Orlando. It sounded like they lived next to each other there.

They'd driven up for the day, a four-hour roundtrip pilgrimage they completed at least once each year. Usually their husbands accompanied them, but this morning the men had opted to complete one last round of golf before the weather washed them out.

"Did you have someone who fought here?" I asked casually.

Mabel shook her head. "No, it's just that being in The Villages all winter, it's the closest battlefield we can get to down here."

"Are you Civil War buffs?" I pressed.

"War Between the States," Caroline corrected quickly. "And if Herbert was here, he'd call it the War of Northern Aggression."

"Well, I did notice the bumper sticker," I confessed.

"Oh that, that's just a joke." Mabel chuckled. "We only travel between Charleston and here, so it's not like we ever drive through Massachusetts or some such. We didn't have an ancestor who fought here, but we do have Confederate ancestors."

"As does Herbert," Caroline added with a nod. "A lot of people don't realize this, but almost half of all Southern whites have at least one ancestor who fought for the Confederacy."

I admitted that was news to me.

"Much higher percentage than up North," Caroline continued. "It may have been that high at one time, but the descendants of Northern veterans have been diluted by all that immigration they had up there after the War."

I had my opening. "Do you think that's the reason the War seems so much more important down South?"

The sisters paused and looked at each other before shrugging.

"I wouldn't think so," Mabel said. "It may be a smaller percentage of Northerners who claim an ancestor, but that wouldn't affect the raw numbers."

"There are five times as many members of the Sons of Confederate Veterans than there are members of that Northern group," Caroline added. "Yet the number of descendants of veterans should be about the same, North and South."

Mabel nodded. "I think the interest for us is really because of the traumatic effect the War had on us."

"Us?"

"If you grew up in the North," Caroline explained, "you probably hardly ever think of the War. But down here, it was fought in our backyard. At least, for the most part. When you're raised in the South, there's always a battlefield or graveyard within a few miles. As schoolchildren, you grow up with that, much as I would think that children in France near Normandy would be aware of that. Up North, it's thought of as a distant war, something that happened 'down South,' as they like to say."

"That makes us closer to the stories," Mabel said. "We remember what our grandparents told us about the effects. They were just one generation removed and heard the details from their parents. You know, the families who lost someone, or the neighbor who didn't come back."

"That's another statistic," Caroline said. "Twenty-five percent of all military-age Southern men didn't come back from the War. Every family lost someone or had a relative or neighbor who did."

We stopped at a marker. The three of us read in silence.

"After the war, General Colquitt returned to Georgia," I said when I figured they'd finished. I didn't want them to think me a total idiot.

"It was worse up there—I mean in Georgia. After the War. Everything destroyed, the balance in the country forever altered." Caroline stared off into the distance.

"Balance?"

"The loss of the South's dignity." She resumed her pace. "Respect, power, all resulting from the Southern states doing what every founding father would have assumed they had an absolute right to do—secede."

"You think so?"

"Of course, not one of the original thirteen colonies ever would have signed the Constitution if they thought they couldn't withdraw from it if things didn't work out. The concept of a new central government was too uncertain—they never would have agreed to that stipulation. If the Constitution said they couldn't withdraw, no one would have signed it."

"My husband says it's like these college athletic conferences," Mabel interjected. "Colleges leave all the time to join other conferences. No one goes to war over it."

"What did you mean by loss?" I pressed. "The physical destruction?"

"It was more than that," Mabel explained. "It was a permanent shift in power. A sort of evisceration of the South after the War, like an imposed punishment. You know, of the first twelve presidents, eight were from the South. After the Lincoln-Johnson administration ended in 1869, there wasn't another president from the South until Lyndon Johnson."

"And that was only because Kennedy was killed, and he took office that way," Caroline added.

"That's a hundred years," Mabel said. "Twenty presidents in a row and none from Dixie. Same with Supreme Court chief justices. Three of the first five were from the South. But after the war, only two of the next nine."

"Business, investment, industrialization, all the same," Caroline added. "By the 1930's income in the South was one-half the national average. We got cut off, punished, ignored, made fun of. If we were portrayed on television it was as a bunch of cartoonish figures, like in The Dukes of Hazard, or The Beverly Hillbillies. They wouldn't let us leave, but they wouldn't let us rejoin either. All men created equal, what a laugh!"

"Being a downtrodden, ignored and made-fun-of section of the country gave Southerners a common bond for the first hundred years or so after the War," Mabel said. "A sort of we're all-in-this together attitude. A sense of community, even if it was based on a feeling of common victimization. It wasn't until F.D.R. came along and invested in the South in the 1930's that we began our comeback and rejoined the United States. The T.V.A., then World War II, all of that. That's why Roosevelt's still so loved down here, he made us feel part of the nation again. Heck, do you know that after the War Between the States Mississippi didn't resume celebrating the Fourth of July until 1945? It was a regular work day like all the others."

"Except the Post office would be closed." Caroline nodded.

"Now we've come back," Mabel said. "Businesses relocated here once the need for water power lost its significance. Companies moving from the rust belt to the South every day. And with our renewed economic power has come a renewal of political influence. After a hiatus of one hundred years, six of the last eleven presidential terms have been filled by men from the original Dixie."

"And that's despite the fact that there are more states now, which should make our percentage smaller," Caroline said.

A knowing grin lit up Mabel's face. "You know, the growth in Southern pride the last few decades can be attributed to a reaction to this rejoinder. I suspect that some Southerners pine for the days when we were down-trodden and possessed that sense of community." She paused, taking a breath. "Memorializing the War helps delay the erosion of that special spirit we had for so long. People up North get upset when we display our battle flag. They don't get that it's regional pride. Heck, on St. Patrick's Day the Irish celebrate, chug green beer while proposing anti-royalty toasts, and no one accuses them of being prejudiced, or anti-Protestant."

Pausing again at the next marker, I brought up the obvious larger issue. "But isn't there a difference? I mean, the whole Confederacy and slavery thing?"

It was almost as if they knew this question was coming, and it was Mabel who took it on.

"Slavery?" Mabel stood up taller, pushing her shoulders back. "The St. Charles' Cross, the one everyone up north mistakenly thinks was our official flag, was only a battle flag. It had nothing to do with the Confederate government. If you want to ban a flag as synonymous with slavery, fine, ban the South's official flag. But our battle flag symbolizes pride in those who carried it into battle valiantly for their state, and maybe also symbolizes defiance of how we were treated after the War."

"Besides," Caroline interjected, "what does slavery have to do with us? I didn't own any slaves, and even if my ancestors did, so what? Not any worse than Ben Affleck's ancestors. How can a flag of regional pride be considered racist? There's people in Boston who fly Red Sox flags or sport the team's decals, even on their license plates, and no one says it stands for racism because Boston was the last baseball team to integrate. What does our Confederate battle flag have to do with today?

"Sure, it was hi-jacked during the desegregation struggle in the 1960's," Caroline continued. "We never should have let them do that. We should have ripped our battle flag out of the hands of the Klansmen who carried it then, and the neo-Nazis who carried it in Charlottesville, and the supremacists who carry it today. But the Stars and Stripes flew over every American slave ship that transported slaves to the United States, and no one says that flag should be torn down."

Mabel paused in her walk and turned full to me. "We're a proud people, Mr. Bauman. But we're loyal too. Southerners have always filled a disproportionate number of our military's ranks. But we can have national patriotic pride, and still remember what happened. You see lots of Canadian cars down here, especially in the winter. And you know what words are printed at the bottom of the Quebec license plates? 'Je me souviens,' the official motto of Quebec. It means 'I remember.' Well, if French people in Quebec can put that on their license plates to remember their own heritage, despite their military loss to the English, why can't

168

we wave our battle flag with regional pride? Those French are loyal to their Canada as we are to the United States, but we both remember."

She gazed out through the trees, as if the past was still unfolding before her.

"That's why coming here, and to other battle sites, is not just interesting, but an obligation." She pointed at the next marker we had reached. "Just think, it was right here, where Southern men huddled and pledged their lives and fortunes to preserve a way of life that was all they knew. They risked all they had that day…"

CHAPTER 27

February 20, 1864
Confederate Command

General Alfred Colquitt appeared to be in a better mood.

Captain Mallory stood patiently as the general finished his conversation with a major. The captain noted that the rough-hewn table from two nights earlier now lay on the ground. A lit lantern tilted precariously in one corner of the tent, in clear violation of military prudence, no matter how far back from the front line the general believed he was. Union sharpshooters could be anywhere. He must be confident that the Yankees were in full retreat, Mallory reasoned.

The table had the same set of maps draped across it as during his earlier visit to the tent, and Mallory whimsically wondered if the general traveled everywhere with the same planks.

The major hurried off, and the general greeted the cavalry officer with a magnanimous smile, extending an arm at the same time.

"Captain! How's your company?"

"We've had a mostly quiet day, sir." Mallory moved around the maps, closer to the general. "We have ammunition, and few casualties. We weren't challenged when the Florida battalion flanked the Negroes, although Henry's Union Cavalry is still out there somewhere. Our horses are in worse shape, still recovering from their trek from Georgia." He didn't add that due to a shortage of feed his company's horses had been in recovery when they had still been in Georgia.

"That's good." The general nodded. "This battle is all but over. The Yankees are in full retreat, running as fast as they can, I dare say. General Finnigan wants to pursue tonight and engage them before they reach Jacksonville and the protection of their damn gunboats.

"He wants your Georgia 4th Cavalry to pursue them on our left. Nip at their heels, so to speak, make them turn and defend, and give the Georgia infantry regiments a chance to catch them. Those damn nigger regiments gave the Yankees an almost two hour head start, and catching them in the dark is going to be difficult."

"I understand, sir. My men are ready. We can saddle and—"

The general shushed him with a hand wave. "No, Captain, I don't think so. I just dispatched a message to General Finnigan asking him to reconsider. My men endured a long march today, fought all day after little sleep and no food, took high casualties, and are short of ammunition. They need to rest."

Mallory was confused. "So, my cavalry company won't be advancing tonight?"

The general stepped to the make-shift table on the ground. The captain stood back, away from the lantern's glow. You could never tell with Yankees.

"I want you to do for me what you've done the last few weeks. Be my eyes."

The general pointed at the map. "The Yankees will try to make it back to Barber Plantation tonight. They may not reach it in the dark. They may only get to the other side of Sanderson. They have to be more beat than we are, they're not in formation, they'll have stragglers all over these woods, and they're dragging wounded and cannons with no horses."

Despite the risk posed by the lantern, Mallory leaned closer to the map. "I agree. Sir."

"Pick an aide, someone to give you a bit of help if you run into trouble. He doesn't have to be from your company. Someone you trust. As the 4th Georgia Cavalry advances on our left, cautious for Henry's Cavalry, I want you to move to the right across the battlefield toward the center of the Union Army. Stay hidden, but report back to me on their location, condition, how fast they're moving, and which unit is covering their withdrawal. If they force march all night back to Barber's, they'll be in Jacksonville by tomorrow, and they'll be no reason for us to chase. But if they stop piecemeal, we might be able to pick off some regiments, and maybe get that shot at Jacksonville after all."

* * *

The sun had set a little after six o'clock that day, and the almost full moon had risen a half hour later. By the time Mallory reached the corral, the moon was fully up. A beautiful night for a ride, he thought to himself. Under any other circumstances.

A familiar soldier was feeding carrots to his mount.

"Penniman?" Mallory asked.

The private turned and saluted. "Yes, Captain."

Mallory hesitated only a moment. "Penniman, the general wants me to ride across the battlefield and trail the Yankees. Do you feel like a night ride?"

In the moonlight Mallory saw the private smile.

"I'll square it with your commanding officer," Mallory said. "And then let's be off."

Soon the pair was picking their way east along the northern edge of the day's battlefield. The full moon cast deep shadows. The northern edge of the battlefield was marshy, and those two factors, coupled with their concern for Yankee snipers, made the pair ride cautiously. Getting stuck in the marsh could severely injure an already weary horse. Getting shot was worse.

"You like riding at night, Captain?" Penniman pulled up alongside the officer.

Despite the jovial nature of the conversation the captain noted how watchful Penniman was, his head on a swivel for marsh and Yankee alike.

"I do, Private. I always did."

"This moon is nice, Captain, but you can't beat a Georgia moon in the summer, wouldn't you say?"

"I don't know. Your accent isn't pure Georgian, Private."

Penniman laughed. "My family's from New York, but I grew up in Georgia. I suppose I picked up a bit of my family's accent first."

A mile beyond the Confederate line, the pair turned to the southeast, intent on crossing the woods at a diagonal. There were more than sharpshooters to worry about. As they passed overturned cannons, discarded equipment and smashed caissons, they heard the moans of Union wounded left behind. Were any of them capable of shooting by the light of the moon?

As if mocking his thoughts, Mallory heard a single gunshot from his left. He twisted in his saddle and strained to listen.

"Skirmishers?" Penniman asked.

Mallory shook his head. "One shot?"

Two more followed in quick succession. As they continued through the woods the sound of stray gun shots became regular.

"What did you do before the war?" The captain guided his mount around a smashed cannon.

"I was in medical school, sir. University of North Carolina. Left after war broke out to join the cavalry."

"No inkling to fight for the Union?"

"No, sir. Born in New York but raised in Georgia. Loyal Southern Son."

"Adopted, I suppose."

Two white objects glistened in front of them. As they got closer they saw they were naked bodies. The dead soldiers lay face down, stripped of their shoes and clothes.

"Someone won't be as cold tonight," Penniman mused.

"I think this was the southern edge of the New York brigade," Mallory said. "Those must be New Yorkers."

The trail of stripped bodies continued. The sound of an occasional groan still pierced the air.

"It's niggers, sir," Penniman said. "I think they fought here. They couldn't take their worse wounded with them when they run off."

"There's a road ahead." Mallory pointed to the east. "The New Yorkers and the Negro regiments used it to get here. It runs along the railroad bed and leads to Sanderson, and from there to Barber Plantation, and then Jacksonville. They're probably three hours ahead of us by now. If they don't stop we won't catch 'em, but I figure they'll rest after midnight. We might still come upon them before dawn."

The sounds of stray shots continued.

Penniman raised up in his saddle and twisted around. "Some of our boys must be pursuing."

"Maybe," but Mallory was doubtful. The firing was too erratic.

At the dirt road they turned east. On the open ground they quickened their pace, even trotting for short bursts. When they spotted a lone figure standing in the road Penniman reached for his rifle, but Mallory stopped him with an avuncular hand on the private's shoulder.

"One of ours. An officer."

The Confederate sentry studied the pair as they approached.

"We're tailing the Yankees," Penniman said. "Have you seen them?'

"I've been in these woods for two hours now. I ain't seen none since I been here."

"Say, what's the meaning of all this firing I been hearing?" Mallory slowed his mount. "Yankees skirmishing?"

"Shooting niggers, sir. I tried to make the boys desist but I can't control them."

"What?" The captain abruptly reined in his horse. "You mean wounded ones?"

"That don't seem right somehow," Penniman added.

"That's so, sir, but one young fellow over yonder told me niggers killed his brother in battle. He was only twenty-three years old, so he was fixing to kill twenty-three niggers, one for each year of his brother's life. He's got nineteen so far, so he only needs four more. I told him to go ahead and finish the job."

Mallory hesitated, and then drove his heels into his horse, leaving the Confederate officer behind. Penniman trotted until he caught up.

"I heard this before," Penniman said.

"What?"

"Today. I was talking to a fellow in Company C in the 2nd Florida Cavalry. He said that before the battle began this morning that their commander, Colonel McCormick, why he rode right to the middle of the regiment, done pull off his hat and stood tall in his saddle. He said, plain as day, 'Comrades and soldiers of the 2nd Florida Cavalry, we are going into this fight to win. Although we are fighting five or six to one, we will die but never surrender. General Seymour's army is made up largely of Negroes from Georgia and South Carolina who have come to steal, pillage, run over the state and murder, kill and rape our wives, daughters and sweethearts. Let's teach them a lesson. I shall not take any Negro prisoners in this fight.'"

"He said that? Are you sure?"

"Lord's truth."

"Two days ago, at the corral at Camp Beauregard, you told me that before y'all marched down here that Colonel Clinch told you that an army of thirty thousand niggers was marching on Lake City."

"He did, sir. Yes, he did say that," Penniman said. "But Colonel Clinch, he never said what we should do if we caught them. I guess the boys are just deciding that for themselves."

CHAPTER 28

Corporal Cotton gently lowered Charles Dunhill to the ground, resting his back against the trunk of a thick pine. Charles winced and placed both hands over his hip.

Thomas squatted in the dirt.

"You can't make no sound. No matter how much it hurts. You understand?"

Charles nodded.

"There be rebs everywhere, 'specially coming down this road," the corporal said, glancing back to the west.

"I reckon we'll hear them before we see them." Charles gritted through clenched teeth. "Though I think them rebs won't want to march too much at night, not after fighting all day."

"That may be true, but that won't stop them from sending out skirmishers, or even cavalry scouts."

Corporal Cotton stood up. "Our troops can't have made it back to the plantation in one night. Them rebs may want another fight, and we be in between."

Stepping back, the corporal moved to the side to let a shaft of moonlight illuminate his fellow soldier. "It stop bleeding?"

He studied the soaked spot on Charles' trousers.

Charles shook his head. "It stop so long as I keep the kerchief on it. But it soaked through good."

Corporal Cotton pushed aside the ragged edges of the trousers and squinted. "It can't have hit no bone, or you not be walking, or standing at all. But we gotta' stop that bleed, and the only way to do that is get that Minié ball out, and then give you a long rest to let it heal."

"Then that's it." Charles grimaced. "We got to keep moving."

Grabbing at the trunk of the pine he struggled to stand.

"We can wait another minute," Thomas said.

"No, we can't." Charles struggled to his feet, one hand still on the tree. "I don't want to have happen to me what happened to my brother."

"Or worse." The corporal placed his arm under Charles. "Here, lean in on me."

Charles placed one hand over the corporal's shoulder while clutching the soaked kerchief to his hip with his other. The corporal turned his friend, and they resumed hobbling.

"What could be worse?"

"That firing behind us. Too many to be single pickets looking for targets."

"You think—?"

"I do," the corporal finished. "Doc Heichold knew. That's why he wanted only us colored on the ambulances. Left his own whites behind. And I don't want me or you to end up like one of them back there."

The pair wound their way through the pines, keeping the moon behind them. The only noise was the four-step sound of the corporal's cadence, the step and drag of Charles' wounded leg, and the sound of the corporal's rifle butt serving as a cane every fourth step. Every few minutes they stopped and listened for an advancing army or scouting cavalry. They heard neither.

"Back home in Pennsylvania, that would be considered a beautiful moon, one for lovers."

The corporal scoffed. "In Virginny it was dreaded. They'd double the overseers patrolling the huts during full moons. That was the most dangerous time for run-offs, figuring we'd want to leave when we could travel at night by the full moon and head north. With the overseers out around the huts all night they'd get bored, and that never went well for the womenfolk."

The terrain rose, then dipped and leveled off. Ahead, the sky lightened as the pair reached the edge of the pines. A road stretched in both directions.

"Is that the one we came down today?" Charles asked. The pain in his hip had dulled, and he'd maintained a steady pace with one hand over the corporal's shoulders. He didn't want to stop.

"I don't know. I can't rightly tell in the dark." The corporal looked back at the moon. "But if so, this road will lead to Sanderson. We might still catch our regiment by morning."

"We can move faster in the road."

Thomas Cotton shook his head. "We be too in the open 'iffen any rebels come along behind. We'll stay in the woods and keep this road on our right."

The pair started off again. Charles concentrated on the skyline as they twisted through the trees. Every hundred yards they paused, rested and listened, grateful when they heard neither hoof beats nor clanking. Charles cringed and prayed at each solitary gunshot.

"The colonel, he didn't make it, did he?" Charles asked.

"No."

"And Major Burritt?"

"I don't know. He was shot up bad."

Charles wanted to cry, but no tears came. "So many men. And it ain't over yet, neither."

"Save your strength," Thomas advised.

"When Colonel Fribley named you a corporal," Charles said, ignoring his friend's advice, "I tell you true, I wanted it. I couldn't understand why he promoted a slave over me who was born free and could read some. And Lieutenant Norton, he wanted me too. He done told me. But now, I see the colonel was right all along. You make a better corporal."

Thomas laughed. "Why, that's the reason the colonel was made a colonel and Lieutenant Norton only a lieutenant."

"At least the lieutenant made it."

Thomas nodded. "I never saw the lieutenant go down. He's a good man."

Charles tightened his grip on his friend's shoulder. "I saw just about all the sergeants go down."

"Well, there you have it. Good thing the colonel didn't make you a sergeant neither. Those red sashes made for easy targets."

As the sky lightened further Charles swung his leg faster.

"If they stopped at Sanderson they'll break camp soon for the run to the plantation. We got to keep moving."

"If they stopped."

The road twisted right, and a field opened before them. The pair hobbled to the edge of the tree line. A hundred yards into the clearing stood a white barn with a two-story farmhouse beyond. In the pre-dawn light they saw a white woman talking to a young Negress in front of the barn door. The white woman carried two pails, and she turned and headed back toward the house. The Negress walked toward the woods carrying a solitary bucket. Charles experienced a momentary panic that she'd see them and call to her mistress, but the Negress stopped and tied the bucket to the end of a rope curled on the ground.

Thomas studied Charles' right leg. Blood soaked the trouser from the hip to the right shoe. He leaned his friend against a tree.

"We gotta' get help."

"We can't, we can't," Charles pleaded. "Doc Heichold be with the regiment. He can take care of the leg."

Thomas looked his friend in the eyes. "We can't wait to catch the regiment. We got to take care of this hip now."

"That white lady will see us from the house."

Thomas shook his head. "Not if we move over and keep the barn between us and the house. You decide, but I don't see how else we cross this field."

"Can we trust her?" Charles asked, nodding toward the Negress now filling the bucket from a dug well.

"She's a slave. We can trust her more than the rebs who'll be coming down this road next."

Charles hesitated only a moment before nodding.

Thomas stepped from the woods and sprinted to his right before turning and approaching the slave who stood holding one end of the rope.

From the trees Charles watched as she stood still, not turning away from the approaching black soldier carrying a musket. Thomas stopped, and the pair stood together briefly, but Charles couldn't hear talking. The Negress turned and dropped the rope to the ground, and together they walked to where Charles leaned against the tree.

Neither spoke but stepped to each side of Charles and placed their arms under his armpits. He draped his own arms over their shoulders and the trio stepped out and retraced Thomas' crooked path to the front of the white barn. Thomas leaned his rifle against the outside wall and unlatched and swung open the rough-hewn door. The three tumbled through the door to the ground inside.

Greg Ahlgren

CHAPTER 29

"Careful, Private!"

William Penniman reined in his horse. Captain Mallory leaned over his mount and squinted at the ground. When his horse snorted and shook its head, the captain patted its neck.

"Two armies have passed over this ground. It's so pitted and rutted that if our horses step the wrong way they'll come up lame."

"Two armies?" Penniman asked.

The captain nodded. "Two Union armies. One marching this-a-way early yesterday afternoon, and one fleeing that-a-way hours later. Dug up ground, rutted wagon tracks, abandoned equipment. We need to go slow."

He loosened the reins and his horse moved ahead, but at a slower pace. Penniman dug in his heels and his horse lurched forward.

"How far you think they got, Captain?"

"Don't know for sure. They got beat up pretty good and are tired, but if they think our army's after them they'll move quick to make Jacksonville."

"If we pick along at this pace we ain't never going to catch them."

"Well, Private, if we go trotting across this ground we'll soon be carrying our mounts." The captain smiled. "I don't suppose that your medical training at the University of North Carolina included horse doctoring?"

"No, sir! Barely began my classes in human doctoring when war came."

"So why'd you quit? Overwhelming love of Georgia, or is there another story to why your family left New York that gives you some special motivation?"

"Neither, sir. It's just, I don't know. Maybe the war was just an excuse. I'd reached that point in my studies where I was no longer sure."

"Sure? About becoming a doctor?"

"About whether I had what it took to save a man."

Both riders reined in at the same time. Through the trees Mallory discerned a lighter patch of ground swathed in moonlight.

"A plowed field?" Penniman asked.

"The Jacksonville road." Mallory urged his horse to the edge of the tree line before again halting. The open road was lit enough to trot over, if it hadn't been more churned and pockmarked than the surrounding woods.

"Every Yankee unit that made its way through these trees came out on this road," Mallory said. "We'd make good time if it was in better condition."

"Sir, if we stick close to the tree line the ground's not as beat. And a Yankee sharpshooter might have a tough time seeing us in the shadows. We'd still have the light in front of us."

"Good thinking, Private."

Mallory swung his right leg over his saddle and dropped to the ground, keeping a tight hold on the reins. "Let's pull the horses awhile. They're panting from today, and we can keep them from taking a bad step."

Penniman dismounted, and the pair tugged their horses in single file easterly along the Jacksonville Road with Mallory in front.

"What did you mean you didn't know if you had what it took to save a man?" Mallory asked, keeping his voice low.

"Not exactly sure, Captain. But when I thought about it, I pictured some fellow injured in a farming accident, all busted up and bleeding, maybe thrown from a horse, and I being the only one there to save him, maybe save the arm too. And his wife and children there, and everyone looking at me to make everything right, and they all thinking I knew how and could do it. I just don't know if I could do that, have a man's life depend on me."

"You find it easier to take a man's life? We've all done plenty of that."

"No, sir. That neither. When I joined they wanted to make me a hospital orderly. I even kept my medical kit in my saddle bags, just to help out in a tough fix, but I think I needed to get away from the whole doctoring field."

Mallory paused, listening.

"Sir?"

"Nothing." Mallory shook his head. "I just want to listen every so often."

An orange haze appeared on the horizon before them.

"We going to follow them all the way to Jacksonville, Captain?"

"If they made it past Sanderson we'll tell the general they're out of reach. If they got that far they'll be on the road this morning, maybe even starting about now, and they'll be in formation for the march to the Atlantic. All our cavalry can do is nip at their heels, like one of your barnyard dogs, Private."

"Well, we haven't caught them yet. No sign we're even close. Doesn't that mean they all camped a ways off, altogether like?"

"Probably. But we still may run into a straggler regiment, maybe even a stray battery that's too damaged to keep up. Something our cavalry could capture. And God knows we could use more big guns, damaged wagons or not."

"I got to pee," Penniman said.

Frederick Mallory took the reins of his comrade's horse while the private turned to the tree line and relieved himself. The sun had risen into full view and the captain squinted and shielded his eyes. It was going to be another clear day.

Penniman returned and fixed his pants. He took his reins back from the captain. "You surprised we haven't found any stragglers or wounded?"

"Not really. The Yankees may have lost, but it looks like they organized themselves and took their wounded with them."

"Except for them back on the battlefield."

"I know." Mallory tugged at his mount again. Around the next bend he stopped. Penniman came up alongside. Mallory pushed his horse sideways into the brush and Penniman followed suit.

"A farmhouse?" Penniman asked.

"I know this farm." The captain jerked his field glasses from his belt and studied the white buildings. "I spent a few days here.

We're maybe a half day's march to Barber Plantation where they were camping."

Penniman scratched his chin. "Well, if they let you stay here they must be sympathetic. You think the owner would give us a good breakfast? That is, if you didn't steal all the chickens when you was last here, Captain."

Keeping his glasses raised to his eyes with his left hand, Mallory pointed with his right.

"You see that barn door, Private?"

"Yes, sir."

"Just outside, to the left. That's a Springfield rifle leaning up against the side of the barn. Here, have a look." Mallory handed over the glasses. "Tell me if that's not a federal rifle. There's at least one straggler inside that barn, and I bet he just might know where the Union Army is."

CHAPTER 30

Samuels-Aggafor Farm
February 21, 1864

The pain had ebbed to a dull throb that only sharpened when Charles repositioned himself against the hay bale. He resolved to remain still, hoping that the lack of sharp pain meant that the wound was not so bad.

"How about a wagon?" Thomas asked. "We could hitch a team and put Charles in the back. If you come with us we could make Jacksonville, even if we don't catch the Army."

Hanna shook her head and dabbed at Charles' hip with a white cloth.

"Miss Aggafor would hear and see us. Even if we got past the house she'd saddle up and come after her wagon. And she can ride fine and she's real good with that rifle of hers."

"How about just a horse then?" Thomas asked, standing behind Hanna who crouched over her patient. "We could gallop past her. By the time she got all saddled up we'd have a good start."

Hanna stopped dabbing and twisted back. "You do much horse riding up on that plantation 'afore you escaped?"

When Thomas didn't answer she twisted back and resumed tending to the wound.

"I thought not. Besides, your friend here can't ride by himself, even if you was on another horse, and held his reins. He'd pitch off before y'all got out of the barnyard. And if you tried to put him up behind you, why, he couldn't hold on none, neither. Even if you could ride."

Thomas grimaced. "What if we took your mistress prisoner? Before she could get her rifle. Tie her up and bring her with us."

"And her mother too?" Hanna raised her eyebrows. "'Cause she's a handful, crazy or not. How far you think you two field hands going to get driving a wagon down the Jacksonville Road with two white women tied up in back? Next farm maybe. Then they'd hang you. If you lucky. You ain't got no Union Army marching with you, Mister, flags a' fluttering, drums a' beating. It just be you two, and this still be Florida."

"We gotta' do something," Thomas pleaded. "You said your mistress does her own milking. She'll be here again end of the day, and where we gonna' hide then? And moving one place to another ain't gonna' work for long. Charles needs help. If I go chasing our regiment by myself I'll never catch them 'afore Jacksonville."

The movement behind Thomas was sudden. The slat door to the barn burst open with one kick, and two Confederate soldiers stood in the doorway. The shorter one held a carbine and the taller a pistol.

"I demand you surrender!" the taller one commanded.

Thomas spun, searching the ground around him.

"You left it outside," the taller one said. "Down on the ground with those two."

Thomas slowly lowered himself to the ground and the two rebels strode to them.

"Damn!" the shorter one said. "It's three coloreds. Two soldiers and a slave."

"Put your hands up!" a voice behind the two Confederates commanded. "All of you, where I can see them."

Charles looked behind the enemy soldiers. In the doorway a white woman pointed a leveled rifle at the middle of the group. He recognized her as the one talking to Hanna at the well.

The taller soldier, wearing the insignia of a Confederate cavalry captain, did not move his pistol or take his eyes off the three huddled on the floor.

"Why Miriam, so nice to see you again."

The woman stepped inside and hesitated. "Looks like our deserter is back. And brought another quitter with him. You both planning on getting work with the Yankee Army?"

The shorter soldier spluttered and twisted to face the newcomer.

188

"Deserters? We ain't no deserters, ma'am. I'm Private William Penniman of the 4th Georgia Cavalry and this is Captain—"

"I know who he is," the woman interrupted. "He's a yellow-bellied deserter that's brought two niggers into my barn. I saw you both come in here. If you were real cavalry you'd have horses."

Keeping the Enfield trained on all five, Miriam Aggafor circled to her left.

"And my own ungrateful field hand helping deserters and nigger soldiers," she spat.

"You got that wrong, Miriam," Mallory said evenly, still not letting his attention wander from his three prisoners. "We listened outside a bit, and watched through the slats, to make sure there was only the two of them. Hanna here was captured by these Negroes and forced to clean this one's wound. She wasn't helping them none."

"Is that true?" Miriam demanded.

Hanna shot a quick glance at Mallory before turning to her mistress. "Yes, ma'am."

"Deserters or no, you're both Southern men," Miriam said, softening her tone. "I suppose you wouldn't lie about that."

"But there's something else you should see," Mallory said, sidling up alongside Miriam. Keeping his pistol trained on the three prisoners he abruptly swung his left arm up, grabbing the barrel of the Enfield and twisting it out of Miriam's hands in one motion.

She released it and glared.

"So, you did bring these two niggers in here. Are they Yankee deserters too? Y'all going to hide together?"

"He's not a deserter," Penniman repeated.

Mallory gestured with his pistol.

"Crawl to the other side of the barn and stay on the ground," he commanded the Union corporal.

As Thomas Cotton scrambled away, Mallory nodded at Penniman.

"That one's wounded. Take a look." He reached out and Penniman handed the captain his carbine.

Penniman bent next to Hanna and pried back the remnants of Charles Dunhill's trousers.

"Can he move any?" Penniman asked.

"He walked in here," Hanna said.

Penniman stopped his examination and studied the slave.

"Walked in? By himself?" Penniman turned to the soldier. "Can you walk, Yank?"

Charles took a labored breath. "I walked here with help."

"How far?"

"From the battlefield."

Penniman twisted back to Mallory. "Looks like the size of a Miniè ball, all right. Just below the hip. Not a lot of skin damage, but the size is right.

"You got this yesterday, at the battle?" Penniman demanded of the wounded Yankee.

Charles grunted. "At the end of the day. Almost over."

"And you walked from there to here?"

"With help."

Penniman whistled. "I ain't never seen a wound from a Miniè ball smack dab in the middle of a limb that didn't shatter the bone. Off to the side, sure, I seen some pass through the flesh or rip it good. But this wound is smack dab."

"How you know it's not shattered?" Mallory kept his pistol locked on Corporal Cotton.

"If it were shattered there'd be more blood, and there's no way he could have swung the leg to walk, help from the other nigger or not."

Mallory moved to where Penniman knelt.

"Can you get it out?"

"Captain?"

"The Miniè ball. Can you get it out?"

"Sir—"

"If you don't get it out the bleeding won't stop. And if you can't stop the bleeding he dies, am I correct?"

Penniman stood and turned to the captain.

"Sir, these are nigger soldiers. They're escaped slaves, in servile insurrection against lawful civil government. We're within the Confederacy here, and subject to its laws. They're subject to hanging if caught, along with anyone who helps them."

"That's not what I asked, Private. You said you still keep your medical kit. These are enemy soldiers lawfully captured. Can you get the ball out?"

Penniman turned away, as if beseeching someone to overrule the captain. When no one spoke, he closed his mouth and shrugged.

"I'll get my kit, sir." He started for the door before stopping and turning back.

"Sir, if the wound and instruments are clean, there's less chance he'll get surgical fever. If it matters."

"What doctor taught you that?" Miriam demanded, unable to keep the contempt from her voice.

"No doctor, ma'am. I didn't learn from a doctor. I went to medical school or started to anyway. They taught that if you keep everything clean, the probe, the forceps, the wound, the risk of fever is lessened. No one knows why, but they say it be true."

"Hanna," Mallory said. "Go to the house, get all the clean linen you can, especially the ones freshly laundered, and bring them back."

"Stop!" Miriam barked. "Hanna, you stay right there. She's my slave, not yours, and I won't have some deserter ordering a slave to ruin my linens to save a Yankee nigger that should be hung anyway."

"Go," Mallory commanded Penniman, who ducked out the barn door.

"Hanna, you go too," Mallory said. When the slave hesitated he added, "Or I'll shoot you, and then this soldier dies anyway."

Hanna ran out of the barn.

"Deserter or no, you are no Southern gentleman." Miriam seethed. "They'll hang the both of you for aiding a servile insurrection."

"Well," Mallory said, "I've just left a battlefield where our side is murdering colored soldiers who fought long and brave for something they believe. Maybe you think the soldiers doing that are the real Southern gentlemen, but I won't be part of it. Besides, I have no reason to believe these are escaped slaves. For all I know they are free coloreds from Massachusetts or some such place. And I don't think either of these men will say different. And I recognize this one, from our trip to Barber."

Penniman returned with a rolled up green cloth. He knelt next to Private Charles Dunhill and spread the cloth across the floor. Shiny instruments protruded from its inside pockets.

"I don't know if I can," he protested to the captain.

"Don't worry yourself," Mallory said. "If it becomes an issue I'll tell anyone I ordered you."

"It's not that," Penniman stammered. "It's just, well, I never operated on a man before. By myself. I don't know if I can."

Mallory barked a laugh. "Haven't you heard about the federals' Constitution?" He gestured with his pistol at the prisoner. "He's only two-third's a man, so you've no reason to fret."

Penniman grimaced. "I'll need help."

Hanna returned with an armful of linens and dropped down next to Charles.

"Someone to hold him still," Penniman explained.

"Corporal," Mallory said, turning to Thomas Cotton. "You're my prisoner. Do I have your word you won't try to escape?"

"Yes, sir."

Mallory holstered his pistol and pointed. "Help hold your friend."

Penniman shook his head. "Captain, you must be from a different part of Georgia than I am."

"I don't have any chloroform, or morphine," Penniman added. "You'll have to hold his shoulders tight, soldier—don't let him convulse or squirm."

"I won't move," Charles whispered.

"Still…" Penniman rolled Charles onto his side.

"Come here and hold the leg still," he commanded Hanna. "Keep the jagged skin apart." He reached back and fished through the cloth, retrieving a long slender prod.

"What's that?" Mallory asked.

"A Nelaton bullet probe, sir. It's the latest in medical instruments. It has a porcelain tip, so if it finds a Minié ball, the lead will leave a dark spot on the white tip. That way we'll know we found the ball and not just striking bone."

"What will they ever think of next?" Mallory marveled.

Penniman fished the tip around the wound before inserting the prod. Charles arched back as Thomas tightened his grip on his comrade's shoulders.

"Easy, soldier," Penniman said.

Penniman moved the Nelaton back and forth before pressing it deeper and repeating the process. He retracted the instrument and examined its tip.

"It's there," he said. "Don't feel like it broke up none."

He reached again for the green cloth and grabbed a long thin metallic instrument with a screw head at its tip.

"Extractor," Penniman announced to no one in particular. "If the ball is still intact we might get it out in one piece."

He pushed the instrument into the wound with one hand, using the linens to stanch the blood with his other. Hanna pressed on the edges of the flesh, keeping the wound open.

"Good girl," Penniman said softly, peering intently at the bullet hole.

He stopped pushing on the extractor and began slowly twisting it.

"I can feel it," he said. "I think it's screwing in."

When Charles recoiled again Thomas hushed him with a prayer.

"You sure?" the Union corporal asked.

Penniman laughed. "Damn it, Yankee, I'm not sure of anything here."

"You're doing fine, son," Mallory said kindly.

"He's a brave soldier," Thomas said, looking up at the Confederate captain.

"I meant the private here," Mallory clarified, nodding toward Penniman.

"I think I got it," Penniman announced. "Hang on."

Still twisting the extractor, Penniman backed the instrument out of the wound. When it came free, he raised the instrument to the light while Hanna applied pressure on the gaping wound that now bled freely. Attached to the tip of the extractor was a Miniè ball.

"What do you think, sir?" Pennmain asked. "I get it all?"

Mallory took the tool from Penniman's hand and brought it to his face before rotating it.

"Looks like one complete Miniè ball to me."

Penniman grabbed the Nelaton.

"Why you going back in?" Mallory asked. "The whole ball is here."

"There might be bone fragments. I've never seen a Miniè ball not smash a bone."

"But he could swing his leg," Thomas said. "We walked down here."

"That makes no sense," Penniman said, again pushing the Nelaton deep into the hip. "Even if the bone didn't shatter there might be splinters that could cause problems later on. Whoa! There's something moving back and forth."

"So, there are fragments," Thomas said. "Can you get them out, Doc?'

"I'm no doctor but I'll try."

"You sure enough a doctor to me."

Penniman pushed a pair of elongated forceps into the wound, wiggling them back and forth.

"Got something."

He pulled the forceps out and held them aloft. "What the...?"

Thomas leaned in. "That's the inside of one of our cartridge pouches. Leather on both sides and lined with tin."

"There you have it," Mallory said. "Did the shot go through his ammo pouch, through the cartridges and everything?"

"I don't know," the corporal answered. "He done took off his belt and left his rifle to walk here."

"You can thank your Union quartermasters for giving you better pouches than we have," Penniman said. "The leather and tin liner and cartridges softened the blow enough to keep the ball from shattering the bone. I'll make sure, but there may not be no fragments."

Ten minutes later, apparently satisfied, Penniman told Hanna to hold the edges of the flesh tight together while he stitched the skin.

"And remember to keep it clean." He wiped around the stitches. "Wash the cloths to make sure they're clean, and then wipe the wound like I just showed you."

Penniman stood. "How we going to get them back?" he asked as he cleaned the medical instruments and returned them to the pockets of the cloth before rolling it back up.

"Back?" Mallory asked.

"We came here to find prisoners to question. We need to bring them back."

Mallory addressed Corporal Cotton. "Where's your Union Army?"

"I don't know. That be the truth." The corporal shrugged. "We be chasing it all night."

"He's telling the truth, Private," Mallory said. "He has no more idea how far his regiment got last night than we do. But they ain't here. Probably the other side of Sanderson, and no doubt on the move early this morning.

"Besides," Mallory added, "I haven't seen any sign that General Finnigan is chasing. He'd be here by now if he was. I think this battle is over."

"So, what are we going to do?" Penniman asked.

"Do? This one can't walk, and we don't have an extra mount. They'll slow us down."

"You're going to leave Yankees here, on my farm?" Miriam demanded. Her eyes flew from the wounded soldier to the captain.

"Even if I had a way to carry them, I ain't taking them back to feed them, or hang 'em, so our work here is done. Yankee cavalry will be looking for stragglers and wounded, so I don't reckon you'll have them all that long.

"And after that," he added with a wink at Miriam, "I might mosey on back myself to make sure everything is fine here at the farm."

Miriam put her hands on her hips and stuck out her chin. "If I don't have extra food for Yankees, I sure enough don't have it for liars, neither."

"Ma'am," the captain said, touching the brim of his hat. He led Penniman outside. Together they walked to where their horses were tied at the edge of the clearing.

Penniman returned his medical kit to his saddle bag.

"You know, Captain, if they find out they could hang us for what we just did."

"Well then, Private," Mallory laughed, swinging a leg over his saddle. "I suggest you never tell anyone what happened here today. Maybe not what you heard happened up near Ocean Pond, neither, least, not for a long time."

Digging his spur into his horse's side, Mallory turned his mount and led the pair up the road back toward Olustee.

CHAPTER 31

New York City
Monday, March 14, 1864

This time Edward Dickerson did not greet his visitor in the foyer. When his manservant appeared in his study's doorway to announce the guest, Marshall Roberts pushed roughly past him into the room.

The manservant glared at the intruder.

"It's all right, William," Dickerson said with a dismissive wave of his hand. "Just close the door."

The servant bowed and backed from the room, pulling the door shut.

"Please," Dickerson said without rising, indicating a chair.

Marshall Roberts had not removed his outer clothing. A newspaper was tucked tightly under his arm.

"It's a disaster," Roberts seethed, still standing. "A total, unmitigated disaster."

"And how are we today, Marshall?" Dickerson sat back in his chair. "Better weather than the last time you graced my home, wouldn't you say? Although there's a pretty good wind blowing out there."

Roberts sat without taking his eyes off his host. "Better weather maybe, but not a better mood. Have you gotten my telegrams?"

Dickerson nodded slowly. "Yes, and I can read newspapers too." He jutted his chin toward the one tucked under Roberts' arm.

Roberts removed the paper and pointed it at Edward Dickerson. "Seymour was a fool, a damn fool. A bloody fool, as it were."

Dickerson straightened up and waited. Better to let the man vent, he reasoned.

"West Point graduate." Roberts spat. "For all the good it did him. He let two amateurs take him behind the woodshed. Colquitt, and that other fellow, what's his name? The Mick immigrant."

"Finnigan," Dickerson offered.

"That's him! Damn fool should have waited for Gillmore to return. He wouldn't have made so many mistakes. They say Gillmore ordered Seymour to stay put until he returned."

"And the way he ran things down there!" Roberts unfolded the newspaper and waved it in front of himself. "I've been in Boston, you should see what they're writing up there."

"Not just up there," Dickerson corrected gently, "the whole Northern press is after the good general."

"As well they should be." Roberts ripped through the pages. "Here it is. This is from the Boston Journal last Thursday. Listen to this, Dickerson. '…A Jacksonville correspondent of the New York Post ascribes the recent disaster to our forces in Florida to the too coddling treatment of the inhabitants by General Seymour!'

"See!" Roberts lowered the paper and looked at his host. "It goes on." He raised the newspaper again. "'On taking the oath of allegiance people were allowed to come and go freely through the lines, and doubtless many spies were thus able to obtain important information relative to the strength of our forces and their intended movements. The impression became general, made by the reports of this class of persons that we should not encounter the rebels in force till we reached Tallahassee.'"

Roberts folded over the page before continuing. "'In the meantime, a vigilant enemy had pushed a strong force ten miles this side of Lake City and formed an important strategic point, an entrenched camp, covering rifle pits. This had been done so quietly, so skillfully and secretly, that our officers knew nothing of it 'til they found themselves in the nicely prepared ambuscade.'"

"I've read the newspapers," Dickerson said. "I know what happened."

"But listen to this!" Roberts thundered. "'Whilst on the march, many companies not having their guns loaded, much of the artillery empty, and with scouts and skirmishers with but a short distance in advance of the main force, our army was greeted with shot, shell, grape and canister and we were in such close range that the gunners to some of our artillery were killed with buckshot whilst loading their guns for the first time in action.'"

Dickerson placed his hands together in front of his face, his fingertips touching, and waited patiently.

"This is the best part." Roberts raised a finger. "'All along the route General Seymour had treated the citizens like friends and brothers, but not one was believed among all who had informed him of the preparations that had been made to receive him at Olustee. Persons claiming to be deserters came in and informed us that there were not five thousand rebel soldiers in Florida—that nearly all had gone to reinforce Johnston, preparatory to an assault upon Grant at Chattanooga. We now know that immediately upon our landing in Jacksonville, Beauregard sent troops from Savannah, Charleston, and Atlanta, and called in all the small detachments General Finnigan had in Florida for the purpose of saving the state.'"

Roberts folded the newspaper roughly and tossed it on Dickerson's desk.

"You can read it yourself."

Dickerson leaned forward and, using two fingers, slid the newspaper slowly back to Roberts' side of the desk.

"I've read it, and more. It's all been reported here. In your absence. Much of that comes from a New York Post reporter."

"Wherever the hell it comes from it's all true," Roberts said. "That damn fool Seymour couldn't run a public house, let alone an army. Damn rebels knew everything. They were waiting for the idiot, and he had no idea. Now we've lost our railroad for certain."

Dickerson raised an eyebrow. "So finally, it's *our* railroad now that it's lost?"

"Of course it's our railroad." Roberts guffawed. "But we'll never get it back from David Yulee now. The whole damn press here is outraged that we tried to capture a worthless state. There'll never be another offensive allowed in Florida. We lost our chance because Seymour is a fool. Yulee wins."

Roberts shook his head. "And now that sniveling Lincoln will have to appease the war Democrats and run as some sort of Democrat-Republican, whatever the hell that means. If he wants to keep the presidency, that is."

Dickerson shrugged. "Perhaps not, Marshall."

"What? About Lincoln?"

"About losing our railroad."

Roberts narrowed his eyes. "What do you mean?"

Dickerson noticed his visitor's wary look. "There are other reports I've been hearing. Rumors. Involving the wounded colored troops. After the battle."

"Yeah," Roberts agreed. "I've heard them too. Massacred, they say. The poor devils."

Dickerson nodded. "You know there are those who suggested to Lincoln that he cut a deal with the rebels. Since they are getting beat, offer that if they end this now and come back to the Union, we'll agree to grant all those involved full amnesty, and even return their property."

"I've heard that. All the freed slaves go back, and the traitors keep whatever ill gotten gains they've made." Roberts sighed. "And our railroad becomes a permanent fixture of David Yulee's."

"Do you really think, Marshall, that after this story about the Confederates murdering niggers on the battlefield becomes generally known, that anyone, let alone radical Republicans, will allow Lincoln to engage in any sort of deal like that? They won't accept anything except unconditional surrender."

Roberts shifted in his seat and frowned. "No, I suppose not. That would be a difficult political sale, even for a snake like Lincoln."

Dickerson smiled wanly and spread his arms. "Exactly, my good man. Seymour may have lost the battle, but what happened afterwards may just have won the war. Our war. Other than Seymour winning the battle, things couldn't have worked out more perfectly for us, wouldn't you agree, Marshall?"

Roberts leaned back in his chair, exhaled, and studied his host. When he next spoke, he did so deliberately.

"You know, Dickerson, I consider myself a tough old businessman. When I hired you I knew you were sneaky, but, a tough old businessman is a softy compared to a lawyer like you."

CHAPTER 32

This afternoon

The rain that started lashing the house at noon had finally stopped. Glancing at my notepad I realized I hadn't written anything for over an hour. Agnes Thornberry and the Dunleavys faced me expectantly in the living room of Agnes' stucco cottage.

"So," I stammered, putting my pen down, "this is how the farm got passed down? But what happened to Charles Dunhill? Did he survive? Rejoin his unit?"

"Whenever I tell the story everyone asks that," Agnes sighed. "Private Dunhill recuperated here for a bit before rejoining his unit. They agreed not to move him back to Jacksonville until he was ready to travel. He rejoined the 8th United States Colored Troops, just before the regiment moved to St. John's Bluff. The 8th stayed in the state as part of the District of Florida, Department of the South, until August 1864. There was a raid in Baldwin in July, but Charles was still recuperating and did not participate.

"In August, the regiment shipped north to Virginia as part of the Army of the James and fought at Deep Bottom and in the trenches outside of Petersburg until September."

"Wow, you know the regimental history," I said, with sincere admiration.

"She does indeed," Bill added as his wife nodded. "After Petersburg, the 8th was involved in battles at Chaffin's Farm and New Market Heights and at Fort Harrison in late September. Then Darbytown Road in October. They were also in the Battle of Fair Oaks at the end of October."

"And Charles Dunhill was back by then?"

"Oh yes," Agnes said. "He and Corporal Cotton were both in the trenches outside of Richmond as part of the Union Siege, which lasted until the following March. The regiment was also part of the Appomattox Campaign in the beginning of April, including the Battle of Hatcher's Run at the end of the month."

"His unit was there when Petersburg fell on April 2," Bill said. "Richmond fell the next day—"

"Or actually, Lee abandoned it," Agnes interjected.

"True," Bill agreed. "Then the 8th was part of the pursuit of Lee right up to his surrender at Appomattox on April 9."

"Wasn't your ancestor part of that?" I asked, turning to him. "The Massachusetts one?"

Bill nodded. "Ah, you remembered. Yes, well, so was the 8th Colored, although you never see them in any of the Hollywood renditions.

"After Lee surrendered, the 8th moved to Petersburg on April 11," he continued, "and stayed there until May when they sailed for Texas. They stayed on duty at Ringgold Barracks and on the Rio Grande until November when they moved to Philadelphia. They mustered out in December."

"That's when he came back," Agnes said.

"Back?" I asked blankly.

The Dunleavys exchanged knowing looks. Agnes laughed out loud before gleefully clapping her hands.

"Back here," she said, unable to suppress a smile. "Both he and his brother, Benjamin, who had survived after all."

I still didn't get it.

"Why?"

"Because of Hanna," she answered.

"Ah," I said. I thought I understood.

"He came back, and he and Hanna married."

I nodded. "Charles Dunhill? Wasn't that a bit awkward? I mean with the Mallorys and everything?"

"The Mallorys?" Alice Dunleavy asked, narrowing her eyes.

"Frederick and Miriam."

"Oh, I have no idea what happened to Captain Frederick Mallory," Agnes said, smoothing a ruffle on her skirt. "I assume he returned to Georgia after the war, if he even survived it."

"So, Miriam didn't marry him?" I stammered, confused again. "Then who did Miriam marry? Who was your great grandfather?"

Agnes shrugged. "As far as we can determine from Ancestry, Miriam never married. She died in 1873 of a fever after returning from visiting relatives in Memphis. May have caught something while traveling. Never married, no children. Her farm passed to her uncle as her only living relative."

I scratched the side of my head. "But if Miriam never married Captain Mallory, or anyone else, and never had children, how can you be—" I flipped over a page of my notes "—her great granddaughter?"

"I'm not," she said simply. "I'm the great granddaughter of Charles and Hanna."

That took a moment. There were so many reasons why it couldn't be.

"But, you're—"

"—white?" She laughed. "Charles and Hanna were both bi-racial. Captain Mallory mistook Hanna for white the first time he saw her. He thought she was Miriam's sister. Their daughter, also light, married Carl Van de Beeken, a local white farmer."

"Perhaps being the sole heir of her own farm may have played a part in Mr. Van de Beeken's liberality," Bill said with a twinkle in his eye.

"Hush up!" Agnes scolded. "You're talking about my grandfather here."

They were obviously all enjoying this.

I wasn't about to be deterred. "But wait. You said that your great grandmother's farm was passed down. If Hanna was Miriam's slave, how was it in any way her farm?" I challenged.

"You forget, Hanna belonged to Jacob Samuels," Agnes said. "Jacob never married. When he got back from the war he was torn up pretty good, barely able to walk, and couldn't ever really care for himself, let alone do much around the farm. He's identified in a later census as a cripple. Hanna stayed on, even after emancipation, and took care of him. A lot of slaves did that, stayed on in place. Where else were they to go?"

"And so he gave her both farms?" I asked. That didn't seem likely.

"Well, she was his daughter."

That one stopped me cold. I mean, I wasn't naïve about that stuff, but I hadn't seen that one coming.

"He knew that?" I asked.

"Of course he knew it," Bill Dunleavy said. "That wasn't secret back then. White owners knew which slaves they fathered. I dare say that's why Miriam played with Hanna when Mrs. Aggafor visited her brother."

"The first time Captain Mallory saw them he commented on how much they looked alike," Agnes said. "He mistook them for sisters."

"Because they were first cousins." Still processing, I placed my notepad and pen on the floor. "Which is why old lady Aggafor confused Hanna with Johnny." What was I ever going to write? "So, your grandmother, the one who told you the stories—"

"Was Hanna and Charles' daughter," Agnes finished.

"And people around here were O.K. with that? I mean, back then?"

Agnes shrugged. "This is Northeast Florida, not Palm Beach. People had enough trouble scratching out a living before the war. After it was over things didn't get easier. I dare say people had more important things to worry about than a white owner having fathered a black slave before the war."

"Which is why you go and plant flowers at the Confederate monument at the battle site," I said, unconcerned that I was overstating the obvious. "You're not planting them for the Confederates, you're planting them for one African-American soldier who was your great-grandfather."

Agnes Thornberry leaned forward. All trace of humor disappeared. "That's where you're wrong, Mr. Bauman. Yes, I'm planting them for Charles Dunhill. And Hanna Samuels. But also, for all who fought here.

"You see, Mr. Bauman, like Bill here I have ancestors who fought on both sides. Although Charles Dunhill fought with the

8th Colored, his father-in-law, Jacob Samuels, my great, great grandfather, fought for the Confederacy. I have ancestors who were Union soldiers, and ones who were Confederate. Ancestors who were slaves, and those who were owners. In that way, Mr. Bauman, I'm a true child of this country. That's what we are today, and we should all try to realize it—those who want the monument, and those who oppose it."

She leaned back in her chair.

"I know in my mind the war is over. But the wounds, Mr. Bauman, the wounds. Sometimes it don't seem like they'll ever heal."

* * *

I drove the first half hour south from Olustee on auto-pilot, unaware of my surroundings. It wasn't until my mind snapped to the Bob Evans road sign—always a potential Florida Highway Patrol hiding spot—that I glanced at the speedometer and eased the BMW to under eighty. The traffic would thicken when I approached Tampa, but Northeast Florida was still green-lighting my brain to skylark.

Agnes Thornberry, Bill and Alice Dunleavy, Caroline and Mabel, all floated in and out of focus—Bill twisting that kepi as he waited to speak, Caroline and Mabel walking slowly along the trail while taking time to patiently explain to a stranger, and, of course, Agnes Thornberry, kneeling and reverently tending a plant at a monument that stood for nothing she revered.

But more than that, it was Frederick Mallory risking court martial by ordering Private Penniman to treat Charles Dunhill, and it was Charles Dunhill, a man not from the South, proud of having been born free, returning to the heart of the Dixie from which his grandparents and mother had fled in the night at the risk of their lives—coming back to live in a state that had tried to kill him, to farm near where they had shot him—all for the love of a woman who felt obliged to stay on that same land in the state that had enslaved her, and care for a father who had fought to perpetuate that enslavement.

That decision could not have been easy. During the war's darkest hours, the vision of his return to the idyllic Pennsylvania farm of his youth must have burned bright. Yet in the end his love for Hanna burned brighter. I wondered about their conversations as he lay in hiding, waiting for his wounds to heal. When did he realize that he loved her, decide that if he survived he would come back, not to sweep her away to the Sennett farm, but to settle and make a life with her here?

Bill Dunleavy's admonitions flooded back. In the mid-nineteenth century soldiers had enlisted, not because it was in their best financial interest, but because their heart told them to. "It's feelings that motivate people, not facts." Bill was talking about monuments, but that's not what churned in my mind. I had dreamed of being a political reporter, perhaps rising to be a columnist or television commentator. The Detroit job was a huge step forward. But I also dreamed of making a family—loving and being loved, knowing and being known. Could I live with the emptiness Anne's absence would create? There would never be another woman in my life like the one I had and, like Charles Dunhill two centuries earlier, I had come to realize it.

Thirty miles north of Tampa I stopped for gas and coffee at The Flying J. Then I reached for my cell phone. I had two calls to make. I called the Detroit Free Press and thanked them for their time and the opportunity to interview. I withdrew my application.

Then I called Anne.

AFTERWORD
AND AUTHOR'S NOTES

If one asked students of the American Civil War to name significant battles from that conflict, it's doubtful Olustee would make anyone's list. In the grand scheme of the War of the Rebellion, the battle has faded from collective memory. Outside the Sunshine State, if mentioned at all, it is usually only in connection with the trivia question asking the largest Civil War battle fought on Florida soil.

Yet had the battle gone differently, the course of the war may well have been altered. The war ended in 1865 when the Confederacy exhausted supplies, funds and manpower. Had the Union's Florida offensive in February 1864 successfully cut the state in half, shortages in beef stock to Lee may have reached critical stage by that summer, and his army might not have lasted the winter of 1864-'65.

Of course, a similar alternative history argument could be made regarding any number of battles across a range of wars.

Since 1977, the battle has been re-enacted every February in a historically inaccurate open field where the public, chewing hot dogs and licking ice cream cones, critiques re-enactors. The local multi-day event includes a demonstration of Confederate howitzers (which now arrive towed behind pick-up trucks), a crafts fair, and the annual Tiny Miss Tots Battle of Olustee contest. It never includes the murder of wounded United States Colored Troops. Rarely do African-American re-enactors participate.

After the battle itself, the Confederates reverently buried their dead. The Union soldiers were left to be eaten "by the hogs... in consequence of which the bones and skulls were scattered broadcast over the battlefield," a returning Union veteran of the battle recounted.

On the shores of Europe, the Pacific, and even Southeast Asia, a concerted effort has been made to identify the remains of American soldiers killed defending our ideals. No such effort has ever been made for those American soldiers who died at Olustee to preserve the Union and end slavery.

It's inaccurate to ascribe this merely to regional feelings. Our federal government has made no such effort either, and one has to question why this battle has settled in historical dust. Is it that the Union's attempted incursion into Northern Florida, motivated as much for political and personal financial reasons as for military advantage, is simply too embarrassing?

The political repercussions of the battle were real. By February 1864 the Republican Party was divided, with radical Republican senators such as Wilson and Sumner from Massachusetts believing that the country should adopt constitutional amendments prohibiting slavery and guaranteeing racial equality. Many Republicans believed that Lincoln could not win in November and sought an alternative candidate.

On May 29, 1864 delegates of this offshoot movement of the Republican Party, now calling itself the Radical Democracy Party, convened in Ohio, and nominated John Fremont for president. This posed the possibility that November would see a three-way fight, with the Democratic candidate benefiting from a split Republican Party. In accepting his party's nomination on June 4, Fremont said he would step aside if Lincoln were not re-nominated.

Not having the Florida convention delegates—the defeat at Olustee assured that the Union lacked control over that ten percent of the population needed to get Florida re-admitted and its votes counted—the Lincoln supporters formed their own National Union Party, comprised of moderate Republicans and war Democrats. They convened in Baltimore June 7-8 and nominated Lincoln. In doing so, this National Union Party (at times variously referred to as the Democrat-Republican Party) adopted a platform that called for pursuit of the war until the Confederacy unconditionally surrendered, a constitutional amendment abolishing slavery, government aid to disabled Union veterans, encouragement of immigration, and construction of a transcontinental railroad.

Despite his demand that Lincoln not be re-nominated, Fremont eventually withdrew from the race. With no electoral votes from the South cast, Lincoln and his Democrat-Republican Party won a resounding re-election in November.

That did not heal the rift within the Republican Party. In 1872, pro-Lincoln Republicans such as Salmon Chase and Horace Greeley formed the Liberal Republican Party to oppose Ulysses S. Grant's re-election. In Cincinnati, this party nominated Greeley for president and Missouri Governor Benjamin Brown for Vice-President. At their subsequent convention in Baltimore in June, the Democratic Party mirrored the action by nominating the same Greeley-Brown ticket, which then ran under a combined Liberal Republican-Democratic Party banner. Although defeated in November 1872 by Grant, that party then morphed into the current Democratic Party.

Would a different outcome at Olustee have changed political history? Given Lincoln's subsequent assassination, that is an impossible question to answer. However, it certainly altered the electoral terrain upon which the 1864 presidential campaign was waged.

Olustee's effect was not limited to presidential politics. It also changed the fates of many who did not participate in the battle.

In the summer of 1864 the Confederates finally turned their attention to extending the rail lines south from Lawton, Georgia. Toward this end they began cannibalizing the rails that ran from Fernandina on the Atlantic, to Cedar Key on the Gulf. This time David Yulee could not stop them in the Confederate courts. Only the end of the war prevented the total obliteration of the line.

Following the cessation of fighting, Yulee, like many central to the insurrection, was held as a federal prisoner at Fort Pulaski while the U.S. government decided what to do with those who had politically aided the Confederate insurrection. Eventually they were released, but not before Yulee was forced to cede back to Marshall Roberts and Edward Dickerson their shares in the Florida Railroad that Yulee had acquired in the Confederate courts.

Yulee had begun the railroad in 1853 with a dream of connecting the Atlantic and Gulf by rail. He was the first southerner to use public funds in the aid of the construction of infrastructure when he accepted grants under the 1855 Florida Internal Improvement Act, designed to develop internal infrastructure. He served as president of his railroad from 1853 to 1866.

Although the Dickerson-Roberts syndicate successfully re-acquired the railroad from Yulee after the war, the line was in deplorable condition. In addition to the tracks being torn up during an effort to extend rail service south from Lawton, the Union Cavalry had destroyed an additional thirty miles of track. The railroad defaulted on its repayment of the Florida Internal Improvement grants, and its assets were auctioned off. At the sale, Dickerson's syndicate bought back its own railroad for approximately twenty cents on the dollar, and then re-established the east-west link.

Yulee himself went on to develop other rail lines in Florida, which opened up the state south of Tampa to economic and population growth. After re-amassing his wealth, he retired to Washington, D.C. in 1880 with his wife. He passed away in 1886 at age 76 and is buried in Washington's Oak Hill Cemetery.

In 2000 the Florida Department of State named David Levy Yulee one of the state's Great Floridians. Both Yulee, Florida and Levy County Florida are named after him.

Olustee also changed forever many who fought among the pines.

Following the battle, Private William Penniman left the 4th Georgia Cavalry and became a hospital orderly. Born in New York in 1843, his family moved to Georgia when he was a child. He survived the war, returned to Georgia, and lived to 1908.

In 1901 he set down for his family his written Reminiscences, which are now housed at the University of North Carolina and can also be accessed online. The description in this novel of Penniman's encounter with a young rebel officer as he rode across the battlefield, who told him that the stray gunfire was from "Shooting, niggers, sir," is taken from these reminiscences. Penniman wrote that the day following the battle he rode back over the battlefield where he saw many of the same Negroes he had seen lying wounded the previous evening. Now all were dead, and he noted regarding their wounds that, "If a negro had a shot in the shin, another was sure to be in the head."

Confirmation of war atrocities comes from other sources as well. In a letter home following the battle, Private Jordan of Colquitt's Brigade, wrote: "...We met with more stubborn negro Regts. They were from Delaware and Massachusetts. The white troops were New Yorkers...The negros were badly cut up and killed. Our men killed some of them after they had fell in our hands wounded."

Corporal Henry Shackleford of the 19th Georgia Infantry wrote to his mother "...How our boys did walk into the niggers, they would beg and pray but it did no good..."

Lawrence Jackson of Company C, 2nd Florida Cavalry, described in 1929 the speech to the troops made by Colonel McCormick that appears in this novel as having been repeated to Penniman by a 2nd Cavalry soldier.

The officers involved in the battle fared better in the post-war. General Quincy Gillmore never forgave Truman Seymour for disobeying him and advancing west from Jacksonville. Gillmore served with distinction in the Union Army until 1865, when he left to resume his career as a civil engineer. He passed away in 1888 at age 63.

It is not known with certainty why General Seymour disobeyed General Gillmore's order not to mount an offensive while the latter was away. Seymour was a veteran of the Mexican-American War, and some have speculated that being war weary, he may have simply been looking for a way to end the rebellion quickly. John Hay, Lincoln's private secretary, described him as suffering from what in the 19th century was referred to as melancholy, but today we know as bi-polar disorder. Seymour's moods were known to lurch from complete depression to wild enthusiasm about his abilities.

Following the defeat, Truman Seymour retreated to Jacksonville, and in the ensuing weeks endured searing criticism in the northern press. He was relieved of his command of the District of Florida in March. However, he worked his way back up into command, and was brevetted a Major General. He was present with Grant at Appomattox Courthouse for Robert E. Lee's surrender.

He left the army in 1876 and toured Europe with his wife, Louisa. There, he furthered his passion for art by painting water colors, many from an aerial perspective. He spent his last years in Florence, Italy where he died in 1891 at age 67.

Confederate General Joseph Finnigan was also roundly criticized following the battle, in his case for not more aggressively pursuing the retreating Yankees. In truth, his men were exhausted, and took the opportunity to scavenge for food and clothing from Yankee bodies. Lee did not think harshly of Finnigan, for he offered him Command of the Florida Brigade in Lee's Army of Northern Virginia, where he served with distinction until the war's end.

A native Irishman, Finnigan spent his post-war years among the Irish immigrant population in Savannah, until returning to Florida to run an orange grove with his wife. He died in 1885 at age 71.

After the battle, General Alfred Colquitt led his brigade north and rejoined Lee's Army of Northern Virginia. In the war's closing months he was assigned to defend North Carolina, where he surrendered at the war's conclusion.

Colquitt returned to Georgia and entered politics. He was elected governor in 1876 as part of the post-Reconstruction white resurgence of control across the South. A fierce opponent of Reconstruction, he was re-elected governor in 1880, and then elected to the United States Senate in 1883 and 1888. He died in Washington in 1894 at age 69.

The 7th Connecticut Infantry Regiment suffered relatively low losses in the battle. It transferred to Virginia and fought in the battles of Drewry's Bluff, Bermuda Hundred, Deep Bottom and at Fort Fisher.

In the immediate aftermath of the battle, Captain Benjamin F. Skinner found insufficient evidence that Private John Rowley had intentionally shot Private Jerome Dupoy in the head. However, the men of the regiment were so convinced at what they claim they had seen that Rowley was arrested. While locked up he suffered from bad dreams and claimed to see ghosts. He eventually confessed to intentionally killing Dupoy in retribution for Dupoy's earlier stabbing him.

Rowley was convicted in a court martial and hanged on September 3, 1864 in Virginia.

Colonel Joseph Abbott's 7th New Hampshire Volunteer Regiment survived its equipment failures at Olustee. In April they shipped north to become part of the Department of Virginia and North Carolina until May, and then were transferred to the Army of the James until January 1865. At that time Abbott was rewarded with command of his own brigade, and on January 13-15, 1865 the New Hampshire 7th participated in perhaps their most notable action when, as part of General Alfred Terry's provisional corps, they landed at the mouth of the Cape Fear River and participated in the Union's successful assault on Fort Fisher. They remained in North Carolina for the duration of the war.

Following the cessation of hostilities, Colonel Joseph Abbott, the former Concord, New Hampshire lawyer and Manchester newspaper editor, settled in Wilmington, North Carolina. He started a Republican newspaper in the city and served one term as a United States senator from that state. Although originally buried in North Carolina, his body was eventually disinterred and reburied in Manchester, New Hampshire's Valley Street Cemetery.

Organized in New Berne, North Carolina and in Virginia during the summer of 1863, the First North Carolina Colored Volunteers was our nation's first regiment that contained the designation "colored." Comprised of freed slaves from Virginia and the Carolinas, the unit's commander was James Beecher, a half brother to his more famous sibling, Harriet Beecher Stowe. However, at the time of the Battle of Olustee, Beecher was on leave up north, and so the unit was commanded throughout the Florida campaign by its second in command, Lieutenant Colonel William Reed. Like the 8th United States Colored Troops, the First North Carolina Colored Volunteers had not participated in any major battles prior to Olustee.

On February 8, 1864, twelve days before the battle, the unit had been re-designated as the 35th United States Colored Troops. Almost all histories of this battle refer to this unit by that designation. However, at the time that the battle was fought, the orders re-naming the unit had not yet reached Florida, and therefore throughout this novel I have referred to this unit by the name that all of the soldiers knew it by at the time.

Although engaged in its first major battle, the regiment fought well at Olustee in support of Barton's New Yorkers. Its actions, along with those of the New Yorkers and the 54th Massachusetts, were crucial in allowing the Union Army to make it back to Jacksonville.

For the duration of the war the regiment fought in smaller engagements in Florida and South Carolina, including Black Creek and St. John's River, and in the Battle of Honey Hill, South Carolina.

The 54th Massachusetts was the most storied African-American regiment at Olustee, already famous for its actions at Fort Wagner, South Carolina the previous July. Following its successful delaying action at Olustee, it too retreated toward Jacksonville. However, on February 21 it was ordered to counter-march back toward the battlefield. The locomotive propelling a train evacuating wounded Union soldiers had broken down, and the men of the 54th, attaching ropes to the cars and engine, manually pulled the cars and locomotive ten miles back to Jacksonville over 42 straight hours, thereby preventing the wounded from falling into Confederate hands.

In November 1864, the 54th Massachusetts successfully routed entrenched Confederate militia at the Battle of Honey Hill, and in April 1865 participated in the Battle of Boykin's Mill, South Carolina, one of the last battles of the war. Their history, from the unit's formation in 1863 through their attack on Fort Wagner, was portrayed in the 1989 film *Glory*, starring Morgan Freeman, Denzel Washington and Matthew Broderick.

Despite its inauspicious start at Olustee, the 8th United States Colored Troops went on to perform admirably in several smaller campaigns, as described by Agnes Thornberry and Bill Dunleavy in Chapter 32, until mustered out in 1865.

It should be kept in mind that this book is a work of fiction. It should not be considered a historical source. If a reader is spurred to do further research on the topic, I have accomplished my goal. Anyone interested in learning more about the battle should review more scholarly works. There are numerous articles that can be accessed online, including the New York Times' and other newspapers' coverage of the Union monument controversy. The State of Florida also maintains an excellent website devoted to the battle.

In addition, a number of fine authors have carefully researched and written much more scholarly accounts of this battle and its aftermath, and those works are highly recommended. Two of many such outstanding books are *Florida's Civil War Battles,* by Stephen Webb, and *Olustee and Florida's Cattle Wars*, by Philip Leigh.

I hope you enjoyed reading this book as much as I enjoyed researching and writing it.

ACKNOWLEDGMENTS

So many good people have been generous in providing comment, suggestions, encouragement and assistance for this book that it is impossible to list them all. However, a special debt of gratitude is owed for the technical expertise on Civil War firearms and armaments provided by Dr. Richard Deveaux, the willingness of U.S. Army historian Nathan Marzoli to patiently answer my questions, the literary input and stylistic advice of America's leading techno-thriller author, Helen Hanson, and, once again, to my good friend Bennett Freeman, whose creative, editorial and literary input has been invaluable. All of you helped make this book possible. To all I say thank you.

ABOUT THE AUTHOR

Greg Ahlgren is a criminal defense lawyer who divides his time between Manchester, New Hampshire, Ogunquit, Maine and Sarasota, Florida. He received his B.A. degree from Syracuse University and his J.D. from the University of Pennsylvania. He has been a criminal justice professor, a state legislator, and a political activist, and has appeared as a featured guest on both national and regional television and radio shows on true crime and historical issues. His books include the alternate history time-travel novel *Prologue,* the international thriller *The Medici Legacy,* and the Civil War novel, *Fort Fisher: The Battle for the Gibraltar of the South,* and together with Stephen Monier he co-authored the true crime book *Crime of the Century: The Lindbergh Kidnapping Hoax.*

Recreationally, Ahlgren has been a licensed private pilot, an avid sailor, and a not-so-avid skier.

If you enjoyed this book please feel free to add a comment or review at the Amazon, Barnes and Noble, Goodreads, or any other review website. Greg can be contacted at GregAhlgren@aol.com, and welcomes feedback from readers.

Other books by Greg Ahlgren

Crime of the Century:
The Lindbergh Kidnapping Hoax
Branden Books
1993

Prologue
Cold Tree Press
2006

The Medici Legacy
Cold Tree Press
2011

Fort Fisher: The Battle for the Gibraltar of the South
Pen-L Publishing
2016